WHERE THE HEART LIES

Amy sets off to join her wildlife photographer boyfriend Mark on the Isles of Scilly, accompanied by her sister's dog Rufus, who she is dropping off with her sister's parents-in-law, Jim and Maria, at Penmarrow Caravan Site. But when she arrives, the park is deserted — except for the handsome Callum Savernack, who doesn't appear happy to have her there. When it emerges that Jim and Maria are temporarily unable to return to Penmarrow, Amy finds herself torn between her responsibilities to Mark, to Rufus — and to Callum . . .

SHEILA SPENCER-SMITH

WHERE THE HEART LIES

Complete and Unabridged

LINFORD
Leicester

First published in Great Britain in 2015

First Linford Edition
published 2016

A catalogue record for this book is available
from the British Library.

ISBN 978–1–4448–3020–0

Published by
F. A. Thorpe (Publishing)
Anstey, Leicestershire

Set by Words & Graphics Ltd.
Anstey, Leicestershire
Printed and bound in Great Britain by
T. J. International Ltd., Padstow, Cornwall

This book is printed on acid-free paper

1

Amy's good deed was beginning to go disastrously wrong.

Rufus whined pathetically as she got back into her car outside Reception, and she gave him a sympathetic pat. She was going to miss him when the owners of Penmarrow Caravan Site took over his care. But if they didn't appear soon, she would miss her flight to the Isles of Scilly.

'Are you sure you don't mind delivering our dog to Ben's parents on your way through Cornwall for us, Amy?' her sister had asked. She had hastened to reassure her — but where were the Penroses now when they were expecting her?

She turned to give Rufus another reassuring pat. 'Don't worry,' she said. 'It'll be all right. It's got to be.'

For a moment, she wondered if she

could smuggle him on board the plane in her hand luggage. But she knew that even a dog as friendly as Rufus could jeopardise the few days' filming of wildlife that was Mark's latest obsession.

She had been thrilled when Mark invited her to join his team on the islands. This was an important step in their relationship, and one she couldn't pass up.

'Right then, Rufus,' she said. 'What do you say to us taking a look around the place?'

He gave a yelp of pleasure as she fastened his lead. The salty freshness of the Cornish air would have been pleasant if she hadn't been anxious about missing her flight. Rufus, though, had no such concerns, and they set off smartly down the slope through the caravans until they neared the bottom. Here, someone had been hacking at the pink campion and feathery cow parsley at the boundary hedge. She gathered some of them up in a damp-scented bunch, because she felt sorry for them lying there on the ground.

Then, turning, she saw a movement among the nearest caravans, and looked hopefully at the man who strode purposely towards her. His wellington boots were caked in mud, and in his hand he carried a strimmer. His jersey looked old and a torn place on his sleeve was beginning to unravel. Definitely not her sister's father-in-law, who she was hoping to see. Too young for a start, no older than his late twenties. He had thick, tousled hair the colour of dead bracken, and a suspicious expression that was unnerving.

'This is private property,' he said. 'There's no right of way through here to the cliff path. And I see you've been helping yourself to the vegetation.'

She glanced down at the bundle of flowers in her hand, and then looked pointedly at his strimmer.

'It's you who's been slashing at the innocent things and not caring how they suffered,' she said. 'You can't deny it.'

'Any reason why I should?'

'As much reason as objecting to me caring about wild things.'

His eyes glinted at her.

'I think it best if you just go.'

She had a moment of doubt.

'This is the right place, isn't it? The board at the gate said Penmarrow.'

In spite of Selina's instructions, she had had difficulty finding it. It certainly wasn't on the beaten track, but perhaps that was its charm for the people who liked to stay here.

'It's certainly not the right place to turn up at the moment. No pets allowed in the caravans.'

'But I don't want a caravan.'

'Then why are you here?'

'I'm looking for the owners. I need to find them quickly.'

'I'm afraid that's not possible.'

'They must be here somewhere. I promised to deliver their son's dog to them, and that's why I'm here.'

'Then you haven't heard what's happened?'

4

'What do you mean?'

'There's been an accident.'

She gazed at him, dismayed. 'An accident?'

'I'm afraid so. I don't know any details. I had an incoherent call on my mobile earlier. They couldn't get back last night. That's all I know.'

'I see.' But of course she didn't. She looked down at Rufus as if he could tell her what to do. This was a stunner, and no mistake.

'And you want Rufus and me off the place?'

'That's about it.'

She turned to go. With Rufus trotting at her side, she hurried back up the slope towards Reception, trying to work out the best thing to do. She would have to be quick making alternative arrangements — if that were even possible at this late stage. In any case, she was going to miss her flight and would need to book another. This was going to cost her.

'Wait!'

She paused. At that moment, the

phone inside the building rang.

'That could be Jim now.'

Dumping his strimmer, he leapt up the steps, at the same time feeling for the key in his pockets. Seconds later he was inside, leaning across the desk to grab the receiver.

'Penmarrow.'

Holding Rufus on a tight lead, Amy followed him. As if all the worries of the world were on his shoulders, Rufus heaved a deep sigh.

She picked up a brochure from the low, round table nearby. She knew that the Penroses had owned the place for many years. She had met them only once, at the wedding three years ago, when she had been the only bridesmaid and Jim had been kind to her. Now, it seemed, they were in trouble.

'You find that brochure interesting?'

She gave a start. He sounded slightly less sure of himself now.

'It seems you are who you say you are. Amy Winslade, their son's sister-in-law.'

'I knew that already.'

His flicker of amusement vanished at once. 'That's reasonable.'

'And you are?'

'Callum Savernack, a friendly neighbour.'

'Not very friendly.'

He shrugged. 'I came over here to check that all was well. Jim and Maria went to collect his sister from Bath yesterday, were involved in a serious accident on the way back, and his sister's injured. Badly, it seems.'

Amy stared at him, appalled. 'That's terrible.'

'She's conscious now, but Jim can't leave her.

'Well, no, of course not.' She thought of Selina and Ben, off on the continent coming to terms with Selina's recent miscarriage, and knowing nothing of this.

Callum's voice deepened. 'Jim can't think of anything else at the moment, which is understandable. And Maria's in shock. Jim broke off the call saying he'll ring back here later. The only thing is . . . '

Suddenly he looked vulnerable. Amy saw that his face had paled, and there was a small scar on his jawline.

The phone rang again. Both of them jumped. He picked up the receiver.

'You wish to make a booking for June?' he said, his voice tense. 'I'm afraid I can't take one at the moment. Very well. So be it.' He put the phone down.

Amy looked through the window at the caravans on their large, grassy plots, all of them on different levels because of the sloping ground. In the spring sunshine, it looked idyllic. She wondered what would happen now.

Callum rubbed one hand across his face. He looked as if was going to say something to her, but then thought better of it.

She moved slightly and Rufus struggled to his feet, looking up at her expectantly, his eyes trusting.

'I'm sorry,' she said.

Callum looked worried.

'I need to lock up here now. I'm due at the sailing club for an important event, and I'm cutting it fine.'

'But, the phone . . . ?'

'There's no alternative, I'm afraid.' He glanced at his watch. 'People must draw their own conclusions when they get no reply. That's all I can say.'

'I'll do it,' she said. 'I'll stay.'

'You?'

'Why *not* me, if I can be useful? I've missed my flight to St Mary's and I'll have to find accommodation for tonight. I need to sort Rufus out and book another flight for tomorrow. Staying here would suit me.'

He hesitated for only a moment.

'You could be useful. Jim will try to phone back, and you can take a message. My mobile will be off.'

'And bookings?'

'None to be taken. You can use a spare caravan, but not the dog.'

'You're saying I should turn Rufus loose to fend for himself?'

'Hardly.'

'Then what?'

'I'll look after him. He can stay here with you for the moment until I get back later. Then I'll take him home with me for the night.'

'But . . . '

'I can even provide a testimonial. The local vet . . . '

'It's not that.'

He looked so concerned that it was hard to doubt him; but Rufus wasn't her dog, and what would Selina and Ben say?

2

Amy's flicker of relief had already decided her.

'I'll stay. Thanks.'

Callum nodded. 'Make use of the phone if you need to make a quick call. See you later.' He turned to go, but then paused. 'There are pens and paper in the top drawer in case you need them.'

'I'll cope.'

As soon as he had gone striding off, she settled herself behind the desk, ready to take calls and deal with anyone who chanced to turn up unexpectedly. She motioned Rufus to lie down at her feet out of sight of the door, which he did with a contented sigh.

She wished she could relax as easily. The accident was a deep concern, but she could do nothing about that. With sudden resolve, she discovered the number of the last caller. Ben had said Penmarrow would be in financial trouble if there weren't enough bookings this season.

Should she?

Why not?

The man who answered sounded suspicious at first, but her experience gained from working at the estate agent's was invaluable; and by the time she replaced the receiver, he was happy to make the booking.

Newquay airport next.

There were no seats available until late next day. She hesitated, put down the phone, and considered for a moment. Then she reached for the telephone directory. She found the numbers for the sailing schedule of the *Scillonian* from Penzance, and for the Land's End Skybus service and made a note of the numbers. But instead of making use of them, she sat upright at a sudden thought. She hadn't phoned Mark!

The call went straight to voicemail. Surprised, she left a message in the hope he would get it before her plane landed. He would try to contact her on her mobile, unaware that she was unable to receive a text message, and he didn't know Penmarrow's number.

What would Mark do when she didn't show up? Head straight back to their base on an outer island, of course, in the hired boat. The long weekend was little enough time to complete the planned programme. He wouldn't want to waste precious time waiting for another flight when she might not be on that either.

To help pass the time, she examined the shelves behind the desk. These contained guide books on Cornwall, and leaflets on all the activities on offer in the county. The top shelf was empty except for a bowl of silk flowers. She thought of her sad bunch of cow parsley and red campion, and then saw that a small, cupboard-like space opened out of the main room. In it was a sink and draining board with shelves above. On the highest one, she found a drinking glass that would do nicely. She filled it at the sink.

'Now you'll be OK,' she told the

flowers as she arranged them in the water and carried them into the main room. 'No excuse now to be drooping all over the place, shedding petals and making the place look untidy.'

She investigated further and found cups, tea bags and instant coffee in the cupboard beneath the sink. There was a small fridge on the worktop by the opposite wall, and in it she found a carton of milk.

She made coffee and carried it through to the main room with the flowers. The phone rang.

'Penmarrow,' she said breathlessly as she picked up the receiver.

'Penmarrow?' said a bewildered male voice on the other end.

'Hello?' She was almost sure that this was Selina's father-in-law. 'Am I speaking to Mr Penrose?'

'Jim. Yes. But I was expecting Callum Savernack.'

'He's not here at the moment. Can I take a message?'

'And you are?'

'Amy, Selina's sister.'

'Ah, yes. The dog! I'd forgotten the dog.'

'He's being taken care of, Mr Penrose. Jim. Please, there's no need to worry about anything this end.'

'But there are problems, you see. We can't travel home just yet, my dear. There's no help for it. We can't expect anyone to . . . Will you tell Callum I need to speak to him?'

'Of course, as soon as I can.'

'Thank you. He'll know my number. Bookings will have to be cancelled for this next week, you see. It can't be helped, but it's a worry.'

Amy tried to sound reassuring. 'Please, please don't worry about Penmarrow.'

He hesitated. 'I simply don't know . . . And my son mustn't be contacted. You'll tell Callum that?'

'We'll look after everything at this end for you,' she promised.

She heard the gratitude in his voice as he said a few more words and then finished the call.

We, she had said. The word had just slipped naturally off her tongue. She was glad to help out for the short time she was available, but Mark expected her, and she had to go as soon as she could find somewhere to board Rufus.

She wished she could get through to Mark. He had come bursting into her London flat a few days ago, alight with passion for the filming project he had been working on.

'What d'you think, Amy? I've got the official go-ahead.' His voice had trembled a little. 'At this late stage, they've commissioned me. I've been talking to Terry and Pete, and they're all set to come, and you are to be in charge of catering.'

'Me?' A shot of joy ran through her that he wanted her with him. 'When?'

'This coming Friday. We'll be based on one of the outer islands and working from there.'

'But . . . ' Her disappointment was acute.

'Pete's getting a boat organised for when we get there. A lot to cover in a short time, so every second counts.'

'Oh, no!'

He looked at her in surprise. 'A problem?'

'A big one,' she said. 'I've taken time off work to dog-sit for Selina, remember?'

'Oh, that. Get someone else to do it.'

She was startled at his offhand tone. 'I've promised Selina.'

'But you said you wanted to come.'

She had been aware of how much this project meant to Mark, and had sounded Selina out rather hesitantly, knowing full well that at this late stage the local kennels would be fully booked.

Her sister had been sympathetic. She was sure her parents-in-law would step in if Rufus could be delivered to them at their place in Cornwall. And that was how this had all come about.

Amy sighed. She ought to try Mark's mobile again, but felt a strange reluctance to do so. He was single-minded about his project, and getting through to him was hard enough face-to-face.

The phone on the desk rang again.

'Penmarrow Holiday Site,' she said, as cheerfully as she could manage.

'I'm Miss Grace Allardyce,' a voice said on the other end. 'It's an emergency. We've got to come to you at once.' Her voice broke. 'Our poor Buster has passed away.'

'Oh, I'm sorry.'

'And we'd like our usual spot down near the hedge. Buster would want that, dear.'

Amy was surprised. 'You've brought him with you before?'

The voice on the other end faltered a little.

'Not like this, not in a little box. Buster's ashes can only be scattered once.'

Taken aback, Amy swallowed. She wasn't handling this well. She was dismayed to hear a sob before the trembling voice continued, 'Thank you for being so understanding, dear. We'll be driving down later.'

'But . . .'

Hearing a car engine and then a door banging seemed like a miracle. Callum came leaping up the steps.

'I think Callum would like a word with you, Miss Allardyce,' she said, motioning him to take the phone.

He raised his eyebrows at her enquiringly as he did so. She shrugged and leaned back in her seat, listening to his words of comfort instead of the firm refusal she expected.

'Ten o'clock tonight?' he said, his voice warm. 'Everything will be ready for you, Miss Allardyce. No, no, that's all in order. I have to be away by eight tomorrow morning, but of course we'll be honoured to be present at the ceremony.'

We? Amy, on the alert now, stared at him in disbelief as he put the phone down. 'Did I just hear you say that?'

He was half-sitting on the desk now, and she saw that his boots had been exchanged for a pair of trainers but he was still wearing his shorts.

'They're good customers, the Allardyce sisters. They like the caravan down at the bottom. I expect it's ready for occupation, but you might like to make sure. They're friends of Jim and Maria. Getting over here early in the morning is the least I can do. You too, I hope. There will be some explaining to do to them afterwards, of course, and they'll have to leave. I'll see to that. Did Jim phone?'

'He wants you to phone him back.'

Callum slid himself upright. 'I'll do that on my mobile. Have you made a flight reservation for tomorrow?'

'I can't do that until I get through to the film crew leader first, but his mobile's not on . . . ' Her voice trailed away at the expression on Callum's face.

'You mean he hasn't got in touch with you, or kept his phone on so you can contact him? He'll know by now that you weren't on the booked flight.'

'There might be a good reason.' But she couldn't in all honesty think of one. Terry and Pete would have phones, even if Mark's was out of order. And how likely was that, at the start of a project that was so important to him?

'I must try again,' she said.

'Then do it.'

She snatched up the phone. The ringing tone cut out to voicemail. She replaced the receiver.

'That's it, then,' he said.

'Not quite.'

'No?'

'I'll have to find a signal for my mobile in case one of the others has left a message. I have to check.'

'Fair enough. Ten minutes should do it. Leave the dog here with me.'

'As a hostage?'

He ignored her suspicious tone. 'Drive back along the lane you came in on, and you'll see a pub on the right, *The Silver Anchor*. Pull in to the lay-by just beyond that. You'll get a signal there.'

Five minutes later, Amy located the lay-by. She clicked on her mobile, scrolled down, and stared at it in dismay. Callum's directions had been clear and the signal from the lay-by was good. No problem there, only that there was no voicemail or text message to access.

She drove back to Penmarrow slowly, hating to admit that Mark had let her down. The door to Reception was closed but Rufus was there on the other side of it to welcome her. His vociferous attention brought tears to her eyes, and she bent over him to hide them as she felt for a tissue.

Callum came out from behind the desk.

'So?' he said.

She pocketed the tissue and stood up.

'Nothing. A waste of time.'

The stern expression on his face softened. 'There's accommodation for you in the nearest caravan. Jim hopes you'll be comfortable there. With the Allardyce sisters here for tonight, you won't be on your own.'

Amy nodded, too dispirited to speak.

'Are you hungry?' he said. 'When did you last eat?'

She hesitated. A picnic on Dartmoor hours ago. There had so much to think about since that it hadn't crossed her mind.

'I'll get us a takeaway,' he said, and was gone.

They ate fish and chips seated on the steps in front of Reception, with Callum using the trough of bright primulas as a back rest. Rufus, sated with his dish of dog food Callum had provided, slept beside them. Callum had brought extra tins, too. He was a man of surprises.

'I needed that,' said Callum, crackling his polystyrene container flat.

Amy finished hers too. 'That was good.'

'Calmer now?'

So he had noticed? She nodded.

He sprang up and took her empty container from her.

'I'll make us a hot drink, shall I?' Amy said.

'Stay right where you are. I'll dispose of these and do it at the same time.

Coffee suit you? Milk and sugar?'

'Just milk, please.'

While he was busy, she leaned back against the wall. Beside her, Rufus stirred, heaved a sigh of contentment, and then was instantly asleep again. She ran her fingers through his smooth fur.

Callum returned carrying two steaming mugs. He handed one to her, and from his pocket produced two bars of chocolate.

'To fill a gap,' he said.

She smiled her thanks.

'Any idea of when you'll get a flight?'

'Late afternoon, I think.'

'My commitments are such that I'm not free to help out here, as I'm involved in sailing championships this weekend in a big way. I'll try to find someone else to step in, but you'll be here at least until the afternoon. Meanwhile, you must tell any prospective clients their bookings aren't wanted.'

She unwrapped her chocolate bar and screwed the wrapper into a tight ball. 'I see.'

And she did, of course, but something stopped her from admitting that she had already taken a booking for June.

3

The phone rang. Amy froze. Then she picked up the receiver. Another booking? Or Mark at last?

She glanced at the clock on the wall. Only nine o'clock in the morning, even though it seemed like much later after her early start. It had been a late night too waiting for Miss Allardyce and her sister to arrive. At nearly midnight, she had almost given them up, when she heard sounds of a car arriving and then the banging of car doors and the chatter of voices. She had switched on the outside lights well in advance, and in their glow the two ladies looked frail and exhausted.

'Can I help you unload?' she had asked in concern.

'We'll just take our hand luggage in with us for tonight, dear,' Miss Allardyce said.

'Then I'll leave you to get settled in.'

'And we shall see you in the morning?'

'Of course.'

Easy enough to say then, and to mean it for the sake of Poor Buster's grieving owners; but when waking early the next morning, Amy had shivered, yawned, and wondered exactly what she had let herself in for.

Rufus had seemed happy as he went off with Callum yesterday evening, his tail waving slowly from side to side. The tall, auburn-haired man and the black dog looked as if they had known each other all their lives. But she had no idea where Callum lived, or what he intended to do with Rufus while he was here early this morning taking part in some sort of ceremony for the remains of Poor Buster.

The twittering of birds outside and a sudden raucous cry of a seagull had reminded her that it was time to move. The sky looked gloomy and uninviting as she emerged and saw Callum's Land Rover.

'Where's Rufus?' she asked as they walked down through the site together.

'Safe and well. I'll drop him off later.'

They reached the Allardyce's caravan near the boundary wall.

'There you are, my dears,' Miss Allardyce greeted them. She wore tight trousers tucked into knee-boots, and in her hands she held Poor Buster's casket. Its red velvet covering had been removed, and was wrapped round his mistress's head and shoulders, making her into an elderly Red Riding Hood. Amy glanced at Callum and saw the amusement in his eyes. She looked hastily away, afraid she might dissolve into nervous giggles.

They started off towards the gate in the hedge. In front of them stretched the sea, slate-grey and calm as they went out onto the cliff path. A flock of seagulls winged their way towards the hazy horizon, and a slight breeze from the sea stirred Amy's hair. The air smelt of seaweed and bruised grass.

Miss Allardyce came to a stop. 'Just here,' she said. 'I think this is the right place for Poor Buster.'

She opened the casket. With a swift movement, the job was done.

Out at sea, the distant haze had thickened now, and to the west a blanket of grey was fast obliterating the landscape. Grace Allardyce shivered and pulled her cloak tightly round her.

'We were just in time,' she said.

They walked back, and then Callum made his excuses and left.

'I'll collect Rufus for you now,' he had murmured to Amy. 'Here, take the key to Reception. I have a spare one.'

And so here she was now, sitting behind the desk and about to pick up the receiver. She took a deep breath.

'Where are you, Amy?' Mark demanded.

'I stayed here at Penmarrow when I missed my flight.'

'I didn't get your message till we got back to base late last night. The sea fog came in fast, and we lost track of where we were.'

'But why didn't you phone some-one?'

'Our phones were back at camp. We'd only gone out in the boat for a swift look round. Then we spotted these Manx shearwaters and went further than we intended. We didn't know where we were. It wasn't our fault.'

She was silent.

'Still there, Amy?'

'I was worried about you, Mark,' she said.

'No need.'

'But I didn't know that.'

'We're OK, just frustrated. No filming in these conditions. Truth is, it's a good thing you didn't come. We couldn't have collected you from St Mary's anyway.'

'Well, no.'

'We'll stay put on Brouma for now. It's uninhabited, and no one knows we're here or we could be in trouble.'

'The catering . . . '

His voice deepened with warmth.

'Lara's here, a girl we met on the plane. Her home's on St Mary's, in Hugh Town, and she's at a loose end this weekend. She's keen to help us out. She'll keep quiet about the camping, too.'

'So you won't need me, then?' Would he pick up on the disappointment in her voice?

'We might be back again soon,' he said airily. 'I'll be in touch. My battery's going down. Lara can sort that for me at her place, no problem. See you.'

She put the phone down and sank back in her chair. Mark was safe. Thank goodness for that. But her relief was mixed with hurt that he should have so little thought for her in all this. And this girl Lara? She mustn't forget that Terry and Pete were there too. She trusted Mark, didn't she?

Lately, she had begun to feel closer to Mark, and that had been good. They had the spring and summer ahead of them, the promise of long days out with Mark's new and expensive photographic equipment. He had filled her in on all the details of that, and how he felt impelled to pursue new filming projects that would make his fortune.

'I might even travel the world,' he had told her. 'Imagine that, Amy. No more hard grind house-clearing and lugging furniture about for other people.'

'It sounds great.'

At the time, she had been pleased for him; but now she wondered exactly how it would be for someone who had no use for small important details like making sure you had all the equipment you needed to keep safe and not be a nuisance to others.

They had first met when she had driven down to Kent to visit her aunt's elderly friend, who was downsizing and had no more use for some large plant containers. Amy was loading them into her car when Mark appeared, keen to be on hand for any heavy lifting.

The invitation to join him for a meal before driving back to London had seemed natural and they had got on well. Soon after that, he had transferred to another branch of Sundown Removals, close to where she worked in the estate agent's and they began to see a lot of each other.

Now, drumming her fingers on the desk in front of her, she thought of the team's flight to the Isles of Scilly from Exeter. How could his battery have run down so soon? In the fog they had been lucky to get themselves back, obviously without a compass, to their base on their uninhabited island. Brouma, was it? At least it had a name.

She had done a bit of research as soon as she knew Mark had booked her in as a member of the team, but she had never heard of Brouma. She pulled one of the Penmarrow brochures towards her and checked the map of the islands inside the back cover. As she had thought, only a few of them were inhabited, St Mary's being the main one with the only town: Hugh Town. Then there were St Martin's, Tresco, St Agnes and Bryher. There was no mention of Brouma: obviously too small to warrant one. It must be owned by someone, though. Were you allowed to land on uninhabited islands? Possibly only for a short while.

And Mark and the team were camping there without permission.

She sprang up and went to the window. Faint shapes of caravans showed through the gloom now, and the trees behind were visible where they hadn't been moments before. As she watched, more things gradually came into focus, until only the outlines of the hedges were fudged.

Suddenly, she felt chilled with the realisation of the danger Mark had been in. Suppose they hadn't found their way back to their uninhabited island? There were miles of empty ocean between the Isles of Scilly and America, and no one would have known what had happened to them.

'Amy! What's wrong?' Callum had appeared from nowhere.

She shivered.

'You look as if you've seen a ghost.'

She gave a shaky laugh. 'Just a sudden worry, that's all: something I can't do anything about.'

'Your friend?'

'Mark, yes. He's impatient to get on with his filming.'

'Even if visibility's bad?'

'Well no, I hope not.'

'Any news about your travel plans?'

'Nothing I can't handle.'

He looked at her intently.

'So what time is your flight?'

'It seems I'm not needed over there at the moment.' She tried to keep the hurt from her voice, but it was difficult.

'Sea fog still?' he said.

She nodded. That was reason enough, it seemed. But Callum had sounded concerned, and that was a surprise.

'Where's Rufus?' she asked.

'Waiting for you in the Land Rover. He needs a walk.'

She was aware that she needed fresh air too, and time to work out what she was going to do next.

Callum picked up the telephone. 'I can give you half an hour before I need to head back,' he said to her. 'There's no wind, so the racing's postponed until twelve at the earliest. So off you go.'

She walked down through the caravans at a smart pace with Rufus trotting happily at her side, and out through the gap that led to the cliff path. Half an hour would hardly give her time enough to climb down all those steps to the beach, give Rufus the chance of a good run when they got there, and climb back up again. So, along the path at the top of the cliffs it would have to be. Confident that the dog knew what was expected of him and wouldn't go running off, she let him off the lead.

Earlier, the fog had come rolling in from the west, but now the horizon was clear again. There was no breath of wind, as Callum had said. The cloudy sky and the pewter-grey sea made her long for sunshine and clouds casting flickering patterns on the water. But life wasn't always perfect. She smiled as she walked on past the place where Poor Buster's remains had been thrown over the cliff. Beyond that, the ground rose steeply. Rufus ran ahead, and then paused to look round for her. He wagged his tail, panting slightly, as she caught him up.

'Come on then, boy,' she said. 'Race you to the top!'

He streaked ahead as she knew he would. Moments later she heard a series of high-pitched yaps. Then she was at the top too, calling to him while the owner of a small dog greeted Rufus with pleasure.

Amy looked at her in amazement. 'You know Rufus?' she asked, as soon as the smaller animal had stopped yelping.

'Know him? He's my new best friend since Callum brought him home with him last night, aren't you, Rufus?'

The dog gave a wriggle of agreement and licked her hand.

'So you must be Amy?' The woman pulled her red bobble hat further down over her grey curls, and smiled in an engaging way.

This was so infectious that Amy smiled back. Rufus had definitely scored a hit here, she thought. The woman's bright presence lifted her spirits, too.

'I'm Stella Williams.' She spoke as if Amy should know who she was. Then, seeing her blank expression, added, 'I'm Callum's aunt. I live in one of the terraced ex-coastguard cottages, next door but one to Callum, just over the hill overlooking the harbour and the sailing club.'

The little dog gave a whine and scratched his hind legs on the path, sending up a shower of dust.

'Far enough now, Toby?' Stella said indulgently. Then she bent to pat Rufus again. His tail working overtime, he licked her hand once more.

She looked up, smiling. 'Care for a quick coffee? It's not far to my place. Why not?'

Amy hesitated. The invitation was appealing. It made sense to find out exactly where Rufus had spent the night, since she was responsible for him, but she didn't have the time.

'I'm sorry,' she said. 'I must head back now. Callum will want to get off.'

'Ten minutes wouldn't hurt, surely?'

'I think it would.'

'You're not frightened of my nephew?'

Amy smiled. 'I don't want to annoy him, that's all.'

Stella gave a chortling laugh. 'I do that all the time'

'But I'm not his aunt.'

'Maybe you'll come another time, then?'

'That would be good.'

'For me too. It's bad for Jim and Maria, isn't it? I know Callum thinks they should call it a day at Penmarrow. Mind you, they're not getting any younger. He should be grateful to you for stepping in.'

'But I have another commitment and I can't stay long.'

'He told me. It's a bad business all round.'

Amy felt a pang as she thought of Ben's parents' business that seemed on the decline. Jim had made it quite clear he didn't want Ben and Selina to cut short their holiday. Maybe Callum would be able to find another person willing to man the phone, and under his orders cancel everything in sight? She could hardly demand to veto this because it wasn't any of her business.

'I must go,' she said.

'He'll be in a towering rage when you tell him you won't stay,' said Stella cheerfully.

'He might have found someone else.'

Stella laughed. 'Unlikely. See you then, Amy. I'm glad we met.'

No one knew another person completely, Amy thought as she turned away. But his aunt would understand Callum well enough to know his reaction to this situation. He seemed a proud and stubborn man from what she had seen of him so far.

Even Rufus was subdued as he trotted at her side. The walk back was already full of memories, and that was strange. She had heard Selina and Ben talk about Penmarrow, of course, so maybe that was why she felt so much at home.

But now she had a decision to make and she knew what it must be. Stella Williams' friendliness had helped her make it.

4

Amy rushed through the gate into the caravan Site, let it slam shut behind her and then, breathless, paused long enough to attach Rufus' lead. Because she had been hurrying, she arrived at Reception with a glowing face. Rufus' tail waved furiously as Callum came down the steps and bent to fondle his head.

When Callum straightened again, Amy saw that he looked troubled.

'Have I been too long?' she said. She glanced around at the deserted site. Only two vehicles were in the car park: her own and Callum's.

'Not at all.'

'Were the sisters very disappointed to leave?'

'What? Oh no. They're still here.'

'Are they? Oh, good.' Her flash of pleasure surprised her.

'Not from any wish of mine, I assure

you. They refused to depart.'

'So where are they?'

'They've taken themselves off some-where for the day.'

From Callum's tone of voice, it was obvious he was not pleased. Amy smiled. She suspected some deliberate confusion and lack of understanding on their part. Good for them, not being willing to be pushed around!

Callum glanced at his watch. 'It's not amusing, Amy. Something will have to be done about them before you head off later this afternoon.'

'Like what? A forcible eviction?'

He frowned. 'There's been no word from Jim yet, and his phone's switched off. He promised to contact me here. I wish he'd phone.'

'Me too.'

She was relieved when Callum didn't ask why. Her sudden resolve to do something about Penmarrow depended on Jim Penrose's agreement, and she didn't want Callum's input before she had time to think it through.

'I'll give you a buzz later,' he said. 'And you'd better have my mobile number in case there are any difficulties. Although what I'll be able to do about it, I don't know.' He took out a card and handed it to her. 'You might have better luck with the ladies than I had.'

'You think so?'

'I can see they've taken to you, Amy. They don't to everybody. They'll listen to what you say, perhaps, and see the sense of it.'

'But think of Poor Buster in his watery grave. How can I upset his grieving owners at a time like this?'

'Now you're laughing at me.'

'Would I do that?' Amy tried to look innocent.

'Poor Buster was a mouse, Amy, not a beloved dog. No doubt he will be replaced as soon as they leave here.'

'And is a mouse any less important than a dog?'

He shrugged. 'I would say so.'

'You think it would be any less loved by its owner?'

'I've no time now for philosophical discussion.'

She smiled, sorry she had teased him. 'Then off you go. I've got things here I have to think about.'

All she needed now was Jim's phone call, and that came twenty minutes after Callum had gone striding off to the car park, the sunshine striking the back of his head.

★ ★ ★

In her job at the estate agents, Amy had a great deal of experience in dealing with the public. She had always enjoyed showing prospective purchasers around properties, and helping them to assess their wishes and needs.

Occasionally, she had helped out at a local art gallery too, and had revelled in the relationship between painting and purchaser. Maybe ensuring that clients were happy with their caravans at Penmarrow would provide the same pleasure to her now.

Jim Penrose had been pleased to hear that her plans for the coming week included staying exactly where she was at Penmarrow. Rufus could sleep and spend most of his time in their house as they had originally planned. Meanwhile, she must be sensible about taking time off, and should close Reception every afternoon. A notice on the door would suffice. With the Allardyce sisters the only occupants at the moment, this should be no problem. And neither would closing Reception at eight o'clock each evening.

'And is it in order to take more bookings?'

'Yes, my dear, and thank you.' He sounded so humbly grateful that her eyes glistened as she listened to what else he had to say.

When at last he rang off, she stood up and looked round the room. With Jim Penrose's blessing, this was to be her domain for the next few days. Noticing that the feathery cow parsley was shedding its tiny petals, she whisked the whole arrangement into the kitchenette and disposed of the dying flower arrangement in the bin.

She hadn't had time to ask Callum what she was expected to do about lunch, but that was no problem. She could last out until two o'clock, and then she would head off to the village of Pentowle and see what was on offer there.

Her spirits rose at the thought of some useful action. Jim had told her where she could locate the keys to the rest of the caravans in case she needed them. They were kept on a row of pegs inside the larder door in their home that was tucked away behind the belt of sycamore and fir trees. The spare key for that was in the bottom drawer of the desk at Reception.

There was already a beanbag in position as a bed for Rufus, and no doubt he would be happy there while she was busy. She would also find a good supply of most things in their home, and she should help herself. She wouldn't do that, of course, because they would need them on their return, and it was easy enough to supply her own wants. In fact, she was looking forward to a shopping trip.

After a quick look round to check that all was well, she went out into the cool morning with Rufus. She needed to know the whereabouts of the Penrose's home to satisfy herself it was really where Jim said it was. She wouldn't be away from Reception for long.

There was a marvellous view from the front door. The sea looked calm and the distant headlands were bright in the receding mist. She sniffed the quiet air, almost smelling the salt she fancied was in it. She thought of Mark holed up on Brouma, and hoped his sea fog wouldn't come sweeping in again as fast as he said it had yesterday.

She heard the ringing of the phone as she emerged from the trees on her way back to Reception, and ran up the steps in time to answer it. She had expected Mark because she had been thinking of him. Instead, she heard Callum's deep voice.

'So you haven't booked a flight?' he said.

'Not yet.' Had he spies everywhere, this man?

There was moment's silence, and then the clatter of voices and the sound of a bell ringing in the distance. Someone said something to him, and she heard him reply in a low, patient tone of voice.

Then he spoke to her again. 'I'll have to go, Amy. Sorry about that. I'll phone back as soon as I can.'

He still hadn't rung by two o'clock, but she wasn't waiting in for him. For one thing, she was desperately hungry, and Rufus needed another walk.

'And that will have to wait until we drive to where we're going,' she told him as he got to his feet and stretched, his paws scratching the bare floor. 'But don't ask me where that is until we get there.'

Where they were going turned out to be a pub on the far side of Pentowle that provided tables and chairs on a grassy patch at one side, ideal for people who turned up with a dog. She ordered pasty and chips for herself, and a bowl of water for Rufus.

A young boy came staggering out with a laden tray.

'New round these parts, are you?' he asked with interest.

'You could say that,' she said. 'And desperately hungry for that massive plateful of food you've brought. And you?'

He looked surprised. 'Me?'

'Do you come from round here?'

'I went to London once. And Paris on a school trip.'

'Sounds good.' Amy placed the bowl of water on the ground beside her seat and Rufus began to lap noisily.

The boy looked at the dog with interest as if he had never seen one drink before.

'I saw him last night when Callum brought him home.'

'You did?'

'Yeah, I live in one of the old cottages up there on the cliff with my Mum and Dad. Until Friday, anyway. My grandad was a fisherman, but Dad's given up the boat now they've got the shop.'

'I see.' Amy began to eat her pasty. 'So you'll know Callum's aunt as well?'

'Yeah. She's my auntie too. She doesn't want to be living there for long, either.'

'No?'

'She wants out. Callum thinks she won't get a place of her own big enough for what she wants. It has to be somewhere quiet, really quiet. Mum and Dad think she should go on saving up like they did to get the shop.'

'The one in the village?'

'Yeah. That one. We supply the sailing club with our pasties. That's what I do, deliver pasties. I'm only helping out here because they're short-staffed and extra-busy this week with the sailing.'

'Because of the championships? I

thought I'd go and take a look.'

'Leave your car here, then. You can walk. It's not far. Yeah, the boss won't mind.'

'I'll call in again for a coffee and another of these delicious pasties.'

He looked pleased. 'Glad you like them. So you're at Penmarrow, then?'

'How do you know that?'

He tapped the side of his head.

'Useful to know what's going on. Jim Penrose phoned my mum. He wanted her to do some cleaning up there, but she's had to say no. Too busy here, see, this week?'

He looked cheerful, a short boy with dark hair and intelligent eyes. Too young, surely, to be working full-time?

'I was just thinking that you seem very young, Jason,' she said.

It was his turn to look surprised. 'How d'you know my name?'

Laughing, she indicated the front of his T-shirt. 'I find it useful to know who everyone is.'

He grinned. 'Oh, this. They make me

wear it for work because it's got my name on it. If I tell you how old I am, you'll say I'm small for my age.'

'And are you?'

'Yeah, sort of. I'm useful in a light wind.'

For a moment she was puzzled. Then she brightened.

'Oh, you sometimes take part in the sailing races?'

'They need heavier crews in strong winds. They don't pick me.'

'But there are no strong winds now, and they haven't picked you.'

He looked at her pityingly. 'That's because Lasers are singlehanded sailing dinghies. Laser Championships, see?'

'Oh.' She smiled ruefully, afraid of saying anything else that would show up her ignorance.

A door banged open behind them. 'Jason Williams, get in here at once!'

'I'd better go.'

'Me too,' she said. Smiling, she went with him into the dim interior to pay her bill.

She felt cheered by the encounter and also with the friendly reception she had from the elderly woman who had summoned the boy. Though Jason was adept at not answering questions, he still gave out a lot of information.

'By all means leave your car here, my love,' the woman said to her as she took her money and rang open the till. 'Take no notice of the rubbish this boy talks. No one else does.'

He had given her food for thought, though, and as she and Rufus walked down the rest of the way, Amy wondered what a boy like Jason was doing at his age, working in a shop that made pasties and appearing to be having the time of his life. What was he . . . sixteen, seventeen?

So already she had made contacts, all of them interesting. Mark, of course, would be engrossed solely in his filming project, hardly noticing anyone else. Even Terry and Pete would, to him, be background figures. There was Lara, of course, back on their remote island waiting for their return to base. But of course she might have been invited to go with them in the boat to keep a weather eye on things and look after the compass.

Amy took a deep, painful breath, filled with such a sudden longing for Mark that she had to stop for a moment and lean on the low stone wall in front of one of the cottages. What was she doing here in this place, getting involved with people who so recently had been strangers to her? Madness, utter madness. She should have scoured the countryside for kennels that would take Rufus, and then got herself over to the islands.

Rufus was looking up at her expectantly, and she swallowed the lump in her throat She knew she was being ridiculous, but how could she help it? By the end of the week, when Maria Penrose was back, and perhaps Jim too, she would be free to leave Penmarrow and go to Mark. There was a good chance that he was too involved with his project to want to give up on it now, and would be sure to be back there anxious for completion.

'It's all right,' she told Rufus as they began to move off again. 'Just a glitch. It won't happen again.'

She reached the shop in the village square, but there was no sign of the bustling harbour she had expected. She walked on a little further. To the right was a mound of grassy sand and a wide-open gateway. A dusty track wound round some bare ground. Nearby was a sign board, and she went closer to look.

Yes, Pentowle Sailing Club, with gold lettering announcing that visitors were welcome.

She followed the track, and soon saw that it widened as she went round the bend. Ahead, now she could see a line of masts, each with a sail hanging limply. As she watched, a breath of wind stirred the nearest to her, and then the others began to show signs of life too.

People appeared wearing bulky sailing gear, and there were more signs of movement as the breeze gradually strengthened and the flag that had been hanging down on its pole came smartly to life. Suddenly, everything was busy as the boats were claimed and started to move. She couldn't see Callum, but that was hardly surprising in all the activity.

She saw now that beyond this area was a wide, sandy beach, bright with a line of coloured bunting, and with sunlight reflecting off the masts of the sailing dinghies as they were manoeuvred on their rattling trolleys down to the water's edge.

She watched, fascinated, as each in turn was launched, their sails filled with wind, and they were off. Two boys, not much bigger than Jason, collected the abandoned trolleys and moved them up the beach. Already there were dozens there, all huddled together like a game of metal pick-up sticks that some careless giant had discarded. Nearby, seated at an easel and obviously deeply engrossed, was a man in a yellow painting smock and a wide-brimmed black hat.

'Amy, Amy! Over here, dear.'

She swung round. The Allardyce sisters, huddled in their bulky anoraks, were waving to her with enthusiasm.

She smiled to see them. Rufus pricked up his ears, his tail wagging as they walked towards them.

'Where did you find the dog?' Belinda Allardyce asked, retreating a pace or two.

'You'd better not let Rufus hear you say that,' Amy said as she pulled him to her and held his lead taut. 'I'm looking after him until the Penroses get back.'

Grace Allardyce looked surprised.

'Jim and Maria are having a dog at Penmarrow?'

'They agreed to take him for the two weeks while their son and my sister are on holiday. They'll keep Rufus right out of your way, I promise. And so will I.'

'Oh, my dear, that's dreadful.'

'Poor Rufus has nowhere to go, and I simply can't abandon him.'

'That's because you're a kind girl,' said Belinda approvingly.

'We're not used to dogs at Penmarrow, you see,' said Grace.

'Does that mean you'll have to leave?' Amy asked. She glanced down at Rufus, who was watching a strutting seagull with interest. Strange that he should be responsible for seeing the Allardyces off when all Callum's efforts had been in vain.

The two ladies stood like statues. Then Grace Allardyce smiled kindly at her.

'No, no, dear. We shall match your kindness with ours. Maria's our old school friend. We won't let her down.'

Amy smiled. 'Then we're in this together.'

'That is so.' Belinda looked pleased. 'And we've some news for you, We know someone who is looking for accommodation. A caravan at Penmarrow would be ideal.'

Grace Allardyce looked enthusiastic too. 'A wonderful artist,' she said. 'He exhibits in lots of places, doesn't he, Belinda? Such a coincidence to meet him here. What do you say?'

What would Callum say? That was Amy's first thought. She hadn't yet told him about the rebooking of the one he had cancelled. But what did that matter? Jim had given permission for her to take more bookings.

'The caravans are large for just one person,' she said.

'He likes to spread around, and Phoebe will be there, too.' Grace looked round, but no yellow-smocked artist at work was to be seen. 'Oh. He's gone.'

'Phoebe?'

'Didn't you see her — a tall girl, slender?' Grace heaved a deep sigh. 'His sister, you know. Younger than him, of course.'

'I see.' Amy smiled, wondering why she had added the last two words. Or did she want to give the impression that this artist was older than she might imagine, and therefore more responsible?

'When would they arrive?'

'Tomorrow morning? We've already spoken to him knowing it would be all right.'

'And they don't mind dogs?'

'My dear, he doesn't mind anything. I'm not sure about Phoebe, but I don't think it would be a problem.'

'Then I must get back as soon as I've done some shopping, and check that one of the caravans is ready for them.'

'And when you've done that, dear, we'd like you to have supper with us,' said Belinda.

'Eight o'clock when Reception closes,' her sister added.

'Things are happening,' Amy told Rufus as they walked back the way they had come. 'Another caravan occupied from tomorrow, and an invitation to supper this evening . . . And soon we'll have to stand by for some angry fall-out from your friend Callum.'

5

For the artist and his sister, Amy selected a caravan halfway between the one occupied by the Allardyces, and Reception. While she went to the house for the key and the bedding needed for two people, she left Rufus guarding Reception. There must be no scent of dog in any of the caravans, and she explained that to him as well as she could. He seemed to smile at her, his tale waving slowly. Then he began to drink noisily from the dish of water she put down for him.

Like the rest of the caravans, the inside of the one she had selected looked slightly tired, with flimsy brown curtains at the windows and matching upholstery that had seen better days. She was glad she wasn't here on a professional basis, measuring up and noting the condition in preparation for handling a sale on the open market. She would certainly be hard put to it to make the accommodation sound attractive.

Opening a window to dispel the musty air before making up the beds seemed a good idea. Then she switched on the appliances and checked that they were all working. The Allardyces were pleased with their accommodation, she reminded herself. She hoped that the new people would be too.

She shut the outside door behind her and walked swiftly back to Reception. She heard the phone ringing, but rushed inside just too late to take the call.

'Pity you can't answer the phone, Rufus,' she said as she sank down in the chair by the desk and reached for the receiver to check the number of the last caller. Mark!

Five minutes later, he rang back.

'Sorry, Amy, a bit of a crisis,' he said breathlessly. 'Just wanted to say things aren't going well. Lara . . . but never mind that now. We want to be back here next weekend if we can. See you then. Oh, and Amy . . . '

They were cut off. Amy stared at the receiver as if it could tell her why; and then, with a sigh, replaced it. *A bit of a crisis* — that could mean anything. She wished Mark had given her some clue. Suppose Lara had vanished when they got back to their remote island? How far was it from Brouma to the main island of St Mary's? Presumably too far to swim. It could be dangerous, too, with strong currents.

Mark wanted her to be there with the team next weekend, and that was good, surely? Yes, of course it was. Still light-hearted with relief, when the phone rang again, she answered with a smile in her voice, thinking it might be Jim Penrose trying to contact her.

But a strange voice replied to her greeting.

'Gabriel Ward,' he said.

'Oh, yes. Hello.'

'You are expecting us at Penmarrow?'

'Certainly,' said Amy. 'Tomorrow morning?'

'Tomorrow's Sunday,' he said.

'That's right.'

'We wanted to book in tonight. Two women recommended you. We hope you won't let us down.'

'Very well. Tonight.'

'I can't say exactly what time.'

'Shall we say nine o'clock, Mr Ward?'

'I'm known as Gabriel,' he said in a hurt tone of voice.

'Gabriel. It would be best for me to have a definite time.'

'But not for us.'

'Nine o'clock will be convenient,' she said firmly. The outside lights will be on. Come to Reception and I'll be there. Nine o'clock.'

'I hope we will, too. Thank you.' He sounded grateful now, and Amy regretted her momentary impatience. She was tired, that was all; and, in spite of her pleasure at being needed next weekend, anxious about Mark, too.

As she got halfway down the site, Amy saw that both the ladies were coming to meet her. Grace smiled. 'My dear, we were afraid you had forgotten.'

'As if I would. I've been looking forward to it.'

'And so have we,' said Belinda gruffly. She was still wearing the baggy trousers from earlier, but she had applied bright lipstick, and plaited her grey hair to hang forward over her left shoulder.

'Your friend phoned just as I was leaving,' Amy said.

'Our friend?'

'Gabriel Ward, the artist.'

'Not exactly our friend, dear. We've just seen him about once or twice.'

'They want to arrive tonight instead of tomorrow morning.'

'That's not very considerate,' said Grace in disapproval. 'Some people expect you to be available at all times, with no thought of what else you might wish to be doing.'

Amy smiled, remembering the sisters' late arrival with Poor Buster's remains in a wooden box. 'Anyway, I agreed. Nine o'clock is the time I told them, so I mustn't be late.'

They reached the caravan, and Amy was ushered inside.

'We'll be as quick as a wink,' Belinda promised.

She set to at once, breaking eggs into a cup, and lighting the gas beneath the frying pan. Soon the smell of bacon and fried tomatoes filled the room.

Grace patted the padded seat beside her. 'Come and sit beside me, dear.'

Amy glanced round at her surroundings, for the first time noticing the many unframed watercolours arranged with precision on top of the fitted cupboards. The white mounts enhanced the subtle shades of the paintings, and Amy exclaimed in admiration.

Grace looked pleased. 'Belinda's own work,' she said. 'All local scenes. Clever, don't you think?'

Amy, agreeing, got up to take a closer look. She recognised a view of the beach that featured in the brochure. There were many charming ones of the cliffs, too.

'D'you do a lot of painting?'

'We were hoping Jim and Maria would like them,' said Belinda wistfully. 'To sell, you know.'

'With a commission for them, of course,' said Grace. 'But Jim and Maria aren't here. So sad about the accident. And poor Jim, with all that worry.'

'But it's so kind of you, dear, to look after us so well,' said Belinda, beginning to dish up.

As they ate, the ladies entertained her with highlights from the holidays they had spent here as friends of the Penroses.

At last, Amy glanced at her watch, hastily finished her meal, thanked the ladies, and was ready to leave.

★　★　★

It was nearly a quarter to ten when Amy became aware of a car approaching Reception. She yawned and got to her feet, not really sure at first of how much time had passed while she was waiting for the artist and his sister to show up at Penmarrow. Rufus was on alert, though, and stood staring at the door, his tail waving slowly.

'A fine guard dog you are, not barking a warning,' she said accusingly.

Smoothing her hair, she wondered why the car door was banged shut in such a peremptory way, giving a strong impression of someone not in the best of moods.

She opened the door as Callum came bounding up the steps.

'What's the meaning of this? You shouldn't still be here.'

Nor you, she almost said in her surprise, but bit the words back. Instead, she stood back to allow him to enter.

He crashed shut the door behind him. 'Why are the outside lights still on?'

'I'm expecting someone.'

'At this hour?'

She indicated the open bookings folder on the desk. He picked it up and then threw it down again.

'Not only are you still here, but you've taken another booking? Are you out of your mind?'

'I'm in charge here now,' she said. 'On Jim Penrose's orders. Or rather,' she amended hurriedly, 'he's happy for me to stay on until the end of the week. In fact, he welcomed the idea.'

'You?'

'Of course,' she said calmly, though she was quaking inside. But what could Callum do to her? He had only to check with Jim to find that out the position. She glanced at the clock. Well, perhaps not now. Tomorrow morning, then.

'I would have put a stop to this nonsense at once if I could have got here earlier.'

'You would not. Jim is happy for me to be here. Relieved, in fact. Why would he want to miss out on bookings when someone can be here to take them for him, and to be on site until he gets back?'

Callum was silent. For a moment he looked so uncertain, standing there in his pale chinos and white shirt, that her resentment vanished. His reaction had surprised her. He seemed to have the Penroses' interests at heart in the way he checked on the place while they were absent, but at the same time was oddly keen to cancel any hint of a booking. A paradox of a man, but interesting, too. All at once, she was anxious for his approval.

'These are people the Allardyces know.'

He looked surprised. 'The Allardyces? You mean they're still here? And who are these people you're expecting?'

'He's an artist. And there's a woman . . . '

'You mean you've taken a booking, and know nothing of any details? They could be anyone.'

'And would that necessarily mean they're crooks?'

'Jim's most particular about who stays here. He insists on knowing names and discovering a little about them. No single-sex parties, for a start.'

'Like the Allardyces? Miss Grace Allardyce and Miss Belinda Allardyce? Two women. Same sex.'

'Yes, well . . . ' His brief smile lit up his face so that for a second he looked younger. She felt too anxious to respond.

'I hope nothing has happened to them,' she said. 'It's very late.'

'Did you take a deposit? How long have the Allardyces known them?'

This was getting worse. She wasn't going to tell him that they had probably not often met Gabriel and his sister, just seen them about the place. He'd have a field day with that.

She glanced at the clock again.

'I shall give up on them now,' she said. 'I'll lock up here, and take Rufus across to the house for the night. It's all arranged with Jim for him to stay there, if you're wondering.'

'I wasn't,' he said, his voice controlled, though obviously with an effort.

Amy picked up the keys from the desk, moved to the door, and stood back for him to go before her. For a moment, he hesitated as if he wanted to say something else. Then he shrugged and went before her into the quiet night.

She switched off the main outside lights, leaving only the low-placed dim ones to light the way to the toilet block. Moments later, the lights from his vehicle were disappearing from the premises.

For a instant, she stood and stared after them, a strange feeling of loss creeping over her.

6

Amy slept late, and the sun was well up above the trees when she pulled back the curtains in her caravan next morning and looked out onto a bright world. At the house, Rufus greeted her warmly, eager for his first walk.

The expected arrivals still hadn't come when it was time to open the office at nine o'clock. As usual, she left the door wide open to give her a good view of anyone approaching along the drive. It wasn't until eleven that they finally arrived, clanking up in their disreputable-looking van.

Both doors rattled open. Even though he wasn't wearing his floppy hat today, Amy recognised the driver as the man who had been seated at his easel near the sailing club, engrossed in painting the heap of boat trolleys. She had thought then how odd he looked in his flowing smock several sizes too large for him.

This morning, he was wearing jeans and a green sweater that exactly matched the colour of his passenger's flowing clothes. Her fair hair was tied back with a long purple scarf, one end of which hung over her left shoulder. Her dangling earrings caught the light as she moved her head. She reached inside the van for her bag, a large canvas affair with a broken zip.

'I'm glad you're here at last,' Amy said warmly as Gabriel introduced his sister, Phoebe. 'Would you like to come into the office for a moment while we sort out the financial business?'

'What about the van?' said the girl. She looked around her, the small lines deepening on the bridge of her nose.

Amy smiled at her. 'It's all right here for the moment. The car park's at the back, hidden away, because that's what the owners like. I'm just standing in for them at the moment.' She hoped the Penroses would approve of these two, who must be years younger than their normal clientele.

Gabriel had already opened the back of the van, and was pulling out a pile of canvasses. 'I want you to take a look at these.'

'He wants to give you first refusal,' his sister said, as if he were granting a huge favour.

Taken aback, Amy watched as Gabriel placed each painting lovingly on the ground. They were certainly striking, and unlike anything she had seen before.

'What d'you think?'

Amy hesitated.

'They all look impressive, but I don't know anything about art.' True enough, although she had enjoyed her temporary work in the art gallery, and was looking forward to becoming more knowledgeable in future.

'Art is the artist portraying what he sees,' said Phoebe, her eyes alight with scorn at Amy's ignorance. 'And by appreciating that we see things differently, too.'

Amy could go along with that. She had never thought of boat trailers in this way before, and suspected that not many other people had, either.

'You'd want your cut for selling them, of course,' he said gruffly. 'Twenty percent? Thirty?'

'But wait a minute . . . ' said Amy. This was going way too fast. Who were these people descending on Penmarrow and seeming to take the place over as soon as they arrived? She was relieved to see another person coming up the path from the cliff now, this time without the little terrier that had picked a fight with Rufus. No stranger, this, but Stella, Callum's aunt.

'Phoebe?'

The girl swung round and flew into Stella's arms. 'Oh, Stella. It's so good to see you again.'

'You've come back here after all that happened?' Stella didn't sound at all pleased.

'How could I keep away from the place?' Phoebe pulled away and scrubbed at her eyes with the end of her scarf. 'Gabriel needed to get away, you see.' Her face clouded. 'A bit of trouble cropped up. You know how it is.'

'I certainly do, where Gabriel's concerned.'

'So I thought of Pentowle. We were so happy at Pentowle. How's Callum these days?' She paused for a wistful moment. 'I didn't know about the championships, you see. They were a total surprise.'

'A big event for Callum and his committee to organise. He's been busy.'

Phoebe shrugged. 'I assumed Callum would be off somewhere else saving the wildlife or something. But this is a lovely place, and it's going to be our base now.'

Stella looked at Amy. 'Is that so?'

'We need to display Gabriel's work for sale,' Phoebe said.

'We'll get you booked in first,' said Amy firmly. 'Then I'll show you your caravan and you can get settled in. You'd better bring the paintings inside Reception for the time being.'

Stella picked up two of them. 'Lead the way, Amy,' she said. 'I'll stick around until the business is done, in case anyone else comes.'

★ ★ ★

'I hope you know what you're letting yourself in for,' Stella said.

She and Amy were seated on the steps outside Reception in the sunshine, each holding a mug of coffee.

'They've booked in for a week, that's all.'

'You don't know our Phoebe. And you don't want to, either.' Stella took a sip of coffee, looked at the stone flower trough appraisingly, and then put her mug down at her side. 'Callum's not going to be pleased she's here, I can tell you that.'

'So what's it got to do with him?'

'A lot, as it happens. They were good together, he and Phoebe. And then there was this huge row when Gabriel got back from his travels one day. No one knew why. They moved away soon after that, Gabriel and Phoebe, and haven't been back since.'

'They lived here?'

'In a cottage the other side of Pentowle. They weren't there long.'

'So why do you think they've come back now?'

Stella shrugged.

'Who knows? But never mind them. Callum said you have some time off every afternoon. Fancy a longer walk with the dogs? We can go down on the beach and watch the boats coming back in. What do you say?'

'Sounds good,' Amy said.

She went back inside to wash the mugs as soon as Stella left. Then she spread Gabriel's paintings out, leaning them against the walls and standing well back to get a better view. What had seemed at close glance to be just jumbles of multicoloured shapes now showed themselves to be several interesting views, including the sailing trolleys from different angles. The design of each was outstanding, and the colours so charming it was hard to take her eyes from them. There were views of the beach, too; though few would ever have seen in it those shades of purple and crimson and lemon-yellow, the effect was magical.

She was so engrossed that she didn't hear a car draw up outside. It wasn't until an elderly couple came through the door, tapping their sticks on the wooden floor, that she was aware she wasn't alone.

The man cleared his throat. Amy swung round.

'Oh, I'm sorry. I didn't see you.'

'And I'm not surprised,' said his wife. 'You've been looking at those beautiful paintings. Are they your own work?'

'I only wish they were.'

'I've never seen anything like them. They're magnificent. Look, Arthur, at this one of the beach. Isn't it lovely? I can just imagine it on our breakfast-room wall. It would cheer anyone up coming in on a dull day, don't you think?'

'Indeed I do.'

His wife took a deep breath. 'Is it for sale?'

Amy hesitated for only a moment. 'Well, yes. The artist has only just brought them in. He'll be back by this evening if you'd like to speak to him.'

'Oh, what a shame. We're on our way home now, and we can't stop. We only called in to see if you had any vacancies for July when we want to come down again.'

Her husband was looking closely at the sunset painting, examining the signature. 'Gabriel Ward. The name sounds familiar. I'd be interested to know the price of this one.'

'That might be difficult . . . '

'May I touch it?'

'Well, yes.'

He lifted it carefully and turned it over to examine the back.

'Ah. Two hundred pounds. That would be acceptable?'

'Yes, of course.'

'What about it, then, my dear? You'd like it?'

His wife nodded with enthusiasm.

'Wouldn't I just? Can we take it home with us now?'

'Of course you can,' said Amy. She had let herself in for something, but who cared? She felt suddenly filled with euphoria that made her senses sing. She would deal with Callum's reaction when it came, as it surely would.

She smiled at the purchaser. 'I'll make out a receipt and find some wrapping paper. The painting's not titled, so we'll call it *Pentowle Sunset*, shall we?'

But the two of them didn't reply. They were too busy admiring their new acquisition.

★   ★   ★

The beach was better than Amy had expected from seeing it briefly the day before. She and Stella, the dogs on their leads, walked briskly past the boat trolleys and the long, low sailing club building with its decorative bunting flying gaily in the breeze. There seemed to be no one about, but Stella explained that the race officers were in the Office of the Day's Hut, watching for signals from the committee boat out there on the water in charge of the race.

'Callum's probably on it too,' she said.

'He's not racing, then?'

'Not this weekend. He has official duties. He took leave these last few days to help get it all organised. A lot to do.'

'And yet he was wandering around at Penmarrow the day I arrived.'

'A report of vandalism up there, that's why. Kids messing about, slashing at the long grass and so on.'

'Slashing things?' Amy looked at her in dismay.

'He knew who they were, and they won't do it again, so there's no need for you to worry.'

Amy bit her lip. She had got Callum wrong. The piles of dying campion and hedge parsley were not the result of action on his part. She had jumped to the wrong conclusion.

They walked on towards the long expanse of silvery sand that stretched right to the high arm of cliffs at the end of the bay. The day was glorious, with plenty of wind stirring the line of dried seaweed that decorated the edge of the softer sand. Beyond that, tiny waves touched the harder part like lines of frothy lace. Far out on the azure sea, the dinghies looked like toy boats.

Amy paused and took a deep breath of salty air.

'It's great to be here,' she said.

Stella bent to let Toby off his lead. Amy did the same for Rufus, enjoying the warm sunshine on her face as she straightened again.

They removed their footwear, tied the laces, and slung them over their arms to carry with them as they made their way carefully through the line of crackling brown seaweed.

'Bladderwrack,' said Stella. 'That's what it's called. What a dried-up mess! You wouldn't think it's so elegant when floating in the water, would you?'

'Where does it all come from?'

'Brought in on storms earlier in the year. It usually gets washed away again, but we've had such a long, dry, hot spell this spring. It sticks around for ages like this, shrinking to half its size. More, sometimes.' She picked up a small piece and looked at it critically before throwing it down again. 'That would have been three times the size when it was in the water.'

'Amazing,' said Amy, impressed. She paused to check on Rufus and saw him running some way off, sniffing. 'I can't see Toby,' she said.

Stella looked towards the cliffs.

'He'll be OK. He likes it over there. And Rufus is enjoying himself, too.'

As they walked up to the dry sand again and sat down to replace their footwear Stella asked if Amy had come to a decision about displaying Gabriel Ward's paintings at Penmarrow.

'The decision was made for me, as it happened,' Amy said. 'You'll never believe this, but I've sold one already,'

'Wow! Quick work. So what was Gabriel's reaction to that?'

'I was a bit disappointed when I told them. Phoebe hardly commented, and Gabriel just looked gloomy.'

Stella laughed. 'That's Gabriel all over. He thinks they're his babies.'

Amy smiled too. They had settled on a commission for Penmarrow of twenty-five percent, which seemed a lot to her, but satisfied the artist. Callum should be pleased with that on behalf of the Penroses, even if he disapproved strongly of what she had done. But why should his opinion matter to her when she believed this was a good thing to do?

Stella stood up and gave a piercing whistle. At once Toby appeared in the distance, and Rufus came loping towards them too.

'The boats will be coming in soon,' she said.

They walked back slowly towards the sailing club. Amy picked up a stick for Rufus to retrieve.

'Not a good idea,' said Stella.

Amy hesitated in surprise. 'Oh. Why's that?'

'I did my work experience at the local vet's. Years ago, of course. A dog was brought in. He'd had a horrible cut under his tongue when he was grabbing at a stick stuck in the ground. I'll never forget that.'

'Nasty.' Amy threw the stick down again. 'So you'd have liked to have been a vet?'

'I didn't get the grades, so that was that. Anyway, I helped there in the holidays sometimes, and enjoyed that.'

The sea was busy now as the boats came in, singly at first, and then in a great muddle of white sails and cheerful shouts. They watched until they were all back and the committee boat came back to shore. Callum was head and shoulders above the rest, and he was easy to pick out among them with his auburn hair glinting in the sunshine. A quick spurt of pleasure at seeing him surprised Amy. Then, with the dogs on their leads, they walked on.

There was a shout behind them. 'Hey, you two, not so fast.'

Moments later, Callum was with them, looking supremely confident in his shorts and T-shirt and carrying his trainers in one hand.

'You're both invited to the celebrations tonight as my guests,' he said, smiling at them. 'Come about nine. Prizegiving first, and then a bit of a social time after that. A few people need to head off, but there'll be plenty left to liven it up a bit. What do you say?'

The invitation included both of them, but he was looking at Amy now, with that searching gaze she found disconcerting. A flush of warmth rose in her.

Stella laughed. 'Just try and keep me away. You'll come, won't you, Amy? It's to celebrate a successful championship. They're always good fun.'

Amy hesitated, Gabriel's mini-exhibition on her mind. Accepting the invitation meant she would be off the premises for some hours when Gabriel might not be there either. He might not have insured his paintings, and she doubted whether Penmarrow's policy would cover any loss or damage. It would be sensible to draw up some sort of agreement for him to sign to indicate that they were displayed in Reception at his own risk. She should have thought of this before.

Amy shook her head. 'I don't think I can. I ought to be on site at Penmarrow.'

Stella gave a scornful laugh. 'Guarding the paintings?'

'You've got a guard dog, haven't you?' said Callum.

'Rufus?'

'That's the one.'

'He'll be in Jim's house. That was the arrangement.'

'Then leave him in Reception. He can earn his keep.'

Stella laughed. 'You're being bossy, Callum.'

'Common sense.' He frowned. 'Anyway, what paintings are these?'

'Penmarrow has a secret weapon,'

Stella said, smiling at her nephew. 'So we can't tell you what it is, can we, Amy? Come on, then, let's go.'

★ ★ ★

All was quiet when Amy and Rufus got back to Penmarrow, just in time to open up Reception. First, though, she took Rufus back to the house, where he drank two bowls of water noisily before tackling the dish of dog food she put down for him.

It was as well she had bought a pasty from the village shop, eaten as she and Stella climbed up to the cliff path, because there wasn't time to cook anything now. It was certainly filling enough, and a coffee and banana now would finish it off nicely. She settled herself at the desk and picked up the telephone.

As she suspected, Mark's mobile was switched off, but she left a message asking him for confirmation that they would be returning to the island next weekend, so she could make a firm booking for the *Scillonian*, the cheapest way for her to get there.

Now she had time to reflect, she began to wonder at her decision not to attend the social event at the sailing club when it would have been so easy to accept. But she didn't know how long the celebrations there would go on, though she suspected it would be long after midnight before they ended.

Outside, nothing moved. The wind had died down, and the sky was grey-blue with a hint of dusk approaching. The silence felt chilling. She wished the Allardyces would return, and that she would also hear the clatter of the Wards' van pulling up in the car park.

She jumped as the phone rang.

'You're not a prisoner at Penmarrow, Amy,' said Callum's deep voice.

'I don't feel I'm a prisoner.'

'I've just spoken to Jim. The notice board outside is sufficient with an emergency number on it ... your mobile number, that is. You'll pick up a signal at the club. Tell the Allardyces where you'll be. That's all that's necessary.'

'I don't think so, Callum. The other people aren't back yet, and I want to be here for their first evening in case there are problems.'

'You're expecting some?'

'Of course not,' she said. 'But I want to make sure. I appreciate your invitation to the celebrations, but no thank you, Callum.'

'Another time, perhaps?'

She put the phone down, hoping she hadn't offended him. But why had she turned down the invitation when Stella, her new friend, was eager for her to accept? Was her sense of responsibility getting out of hand? No, it wasn't that, though it must have sounded like it. As Callum had said, she wasn't chained to the place, and the Allardyces would understand if she had wanted an evening away.

Her reluctance to join Callum at the sailing club was because of something else, something not easily explained

— and certainly not to him. The strange thing was that, even though she felt at home in Penmarrow and Pentowle, she suspected that she was on the threshold of some big change which she couldn't cope with at the moment.

A vision of Callum's tanned face smiling at her came into her mind with a suddenness that was disturbing. She was missing out on an enjoyable social occasion because being in his company was what she feared.

And that was crazy.

7

In the cold, grey light of Monday morning, it seemed even more so. The walk with Rufus before breakfast was shorter than usual because the lowering clouds over the sea promised imminent rain. Even Rufus seemed dejected, keeping close to her side instead of running backwards and forwards on the cliff path investigating every clump of grass.

But as Amy opened up at Reception, the sun burst forth. The clouds began to clear, and by mid-morning, when the Allardyce sisters set out on one of their expeditions, the sky was a clear blue fading to a lighter shade on the horizon. The air felt lighter too, and Amy couldn't help smiling as she set about her task of dusting the shelves on the walls behind the desk.

'That's Cornwall for you,' said

Phoebe as she pushed open the door a short time later. 'Changeable weather from one moment to the next. You'll have to get used to it.'

Phoebe sounded as if she thought Amy was always complaining, and it didn't sound good.

'I think I've done that already,' she said, smiling at her as pleasantly as she could manage. 'Can I help you?'

Phoebe stared round the room, as if she suspected some of Gabriel's paintings had been taken down and hidden away in a cupboard out of sight. She picked an elastic band up from the desk and imprisoned her loose hair with it.

'We're going off out now. Gabriel has been raring to go, but we were late back last night.'

'Anywhere interesting?'

Phoebe shrugged.

Amy had heard the rattling van from her caravan well after midnight, and wondered where they had been.

'Is there anything I can do for you before you set out?' she asked.

'D'you supply bread?'

'Well, no, sorry.'

'Milk?'

'The village isn't far. They sell both in the shop there.'

Phoebe turned swiftly and left, letting the door bang shut behind her. Moments later, Amy heard the van clattering away.

She spent the rest of the morning checking on the remainder of the caravans, and in the afternoon, set off for Pentowle along the cliff path. It felt good to be free to do what she liked for the next few hours.

Ahead of her was the beach. This early in the season there were few people about, and she loved the feeling of freedom it gave her to walk past the sailing club to the wide expanse of sand beyond. The clubhouse wasn't deserted, as she had expected. A band of people were hard at work stacking tables and chairs. She heard cheerful commands coming from inside the building.

She soon saw that Callum wasn't

among the helpers, and that was no surprise. The commodore would be above such things, she thought, smiling. But then she remembered him with his strimmer, helping out at Penmarrow, and the way he had interrupted a busy schedule to keep a check on things because the Penroses were out of action. No, Callum wouldn't shirk physical work.

She walked on. The tide wasn't so far out today, and the thinner line of hard sand gleamed in the sunshine. She took off her sandals to walk barefoot towards the cliffs at the far end, keeping her eye on Rufus, now enjoying himself rooting about among the mass of dry seaweed.

By the time they reached the cliffs on the far side of the beach, even Rufus was flagging. She sat down on a handy rock, and for a few moments he came to sit, panting, at her side. Then he was off again.

She watched him for a while, and then got up and stretched.

'Time to retrace our steps, Rufus, if

you can drag yourself away from that horrible stuff,' she called.

He took no notice and she called again, more sharply this time. When he ignored her, she went to see why he was so engrossed. He looked up at her, tail wagging.

'Come on, Rufus,' she ordered. 'Stop messing about.'

In the distance now, she could see figures down by the water's edge. One of them was in a wetsuit and went running into the sea. By the time Amy had walked across the beach, the person was out again. She saw it was Stella.

'Hi there,' Stella called. 'Good to see you. I've been in to test the waters today.'

'I saw you. Not too bad in a wetsuit?'

'I'd be blue with cold otherwise.'

Amy gave a mock shudder. 'I can imagine.'

Toby came running up, panting, sniffed at Rufus suspiciously, decided he was friendly today, and wagged his tail.

'Feel like coming back with me for a

coffee?' Stella said.

Amy was glad to accept. Rufus was tired too after all his exertions, and walked sedately at her side on the lead as they went through Pentowle to the steep path that took them up to the cliff top.

'What a fantastic view,' Amy said as they reached the top. She could see for miles in both directions, small coves and larger expanses of sand and cliffs fading into the distance.

'Not bad, is it?' said Stella.

Amy glanced at the row of three terraced cottages they were approaching. Built of stone, they gave an air of age and stability that was pleasing.

'Mine is the one this end,' Stella said. 'Callum's is the biggest because it's at the other end. We share a largish garden at the back. It's got some useful outhouses, too. That's where I should be boarding dogs.'

'Is that what you want to do?'

'Callum won't hear of it. He says it's not suitable because it's too near the village down below, and I'd never get planning permission. I suppose he's right, and Toby's happy with the way things are. I look after him for his owner when she goes away. And other dogs, too, but only one at a time.'

Because the dogs were with them, they sat at one of the tables outside. After she had changed into a summer skirt and white T-shirt, Stella brought out two huge jam doughnuts. Rufus sat up and sniffed.

'Not for you, my lad,' she said, producing a couple of dog biscuits from her pocket.

Both dogs munched in a companionable sort of way, and then Rufus lay down and watched the proceedings with an alert air. Toby sniffed around for a bit, and then lay down too.

'I'm lucky to live here,' Stella said. 'Callum's mother had the one at the other end, and I had this one.'

'And Jason's family?'

'The middle one. It'll be empty soon when they move out. You know they'll be living in the flat above the shop?'

Amy nodded and took a sip of coffee. 'I thought you'd be at work today, Stella.'

Stella wrinkled her nose. 'Chance would be a fine thing. I'm unemployed. My firm had to close down. I used to work at Tenbridge Pet Shop in town, advising people on pet care. Now I'm a lady of leisure.'

'But looking for work?'

'Oh, yes. There's an interview set up for tomorrow in a village near Bodmin, up on the moor. There's a craft business with various outlets. A bit too much travelling for my liking, and not quite what I want, but it helps fill the coffers and keep me from starving. I'll be able to put a bit by for what I really want.'

'Need I ask what?'

'A stint in a kennels or something, gaining experience for when I start up my own place.'

'So that's the plan?'

'One day.'

'It's good to have a dream.' Amy

thought of Mark's, that was fast becoming an obsession. Stella seemed more laid back about hers, going about things in a sensible way. Mark had never done that. He had thrown up his job to concentrate on his photography. She would be worried sick if she had done something of the sort. But that was the difference between them.

'So what's your dream, Amy?' Stella put her hand to her mouth. 'Sorry, none of my business.'

She pulled such a face that Amy laughed.

'My dream? I'd tell you at once if I had one,' she said.

'Oh, come on. Think of something.'

Amy was silent for a moment, considering.

'I'd really like to share an interest with a loving partner,' she said. 'Working together for something that's important to both of us.'

'Have you anyone in mind?'

'There's someone.'

'The chap you're going to join over

on the Isles of Scilly?'

Amy nodded, marvelling again at the way that news got round in a small community.

'Where is he exactly?'

'On a small island called Brouma. It sounds great.'

'Do you know the Scillies, Amy?'

'I'm looking forward to my first visit.'

'I've got a book I can lend you if you like.'

'That would be good.'

'Callum goes over there sometimes for his work, and I went with him once.'

'What does he do?'

'He works for the intertidal project team. Coastal work, of course, and he loves it. All that travelling about . . . I like staying in one place.'

Amy thought of Mark again. There hadn't been much chance of supporting him so far. There had been no word from him since yesterday morning, when he had phoned briefly to say that they were making tentative plans to return next weekend, but that was all.

'At least I know what Gabriel's dream is.'

'And Phoebe's,' Stella said, shuddering. 'Didn't we all when they lived here? Callum was lucky to get out of it.'

'You don't like her?'

'You're joking. And what's more, I know her little game. That brother of hers is happy to paint anywhere. He turns out paintings by the dozen.'

'They're good, and it looks as if people like them.'

'Oh, yes. They're good. But it's Phoebe who wanted to come back here. That's plain enough. She's got some devious plan. Just wait and see, Amy. An obsessive pair, those two.'

'But isn't everyone a bit obsessive who has a dream, and is it a bad thing?'

There was a moment's silence. Stella gazed thoughtfully at the end cottage which she had said was Callum's home.

'I sometimes wonder what Callum's got on his mind,' Stella said. 'I know it sounds odd, but I can't help wondering if it has something to do with

Penmarrow.' She stared down at her empty mug.

Amy didn't press it, but she wondered too. She glanced at her watch.

'The time's gone quickly,' she said. 'I'll have to go.

'We'll keep in touch,' said Stella.

Amy smiled as she glanced back at the cottages and waved, before hurrying along the path clutching the book that Stella had lent her.

The sea was a sheen of silken blue, and far out, a lone fishing boat was heading to harbour. At least, that was what it looked like to Amy. But Pentowle's harbour was silted up and long disused, so it wasn't heading for there. Further down the coast, then. She tried to think of where the next safe harbour might be.

Rufus was walking at her side, looking as if he thought they had come far enough on the warm afternoon. By the time they got to the gap to Penmarrow's land, she had to urge him on.

'Come on, Rufus, it can't be that bad,' she said as she waited for him to follow her through.

She unlocked the door of the house. Inside, she filled his drinking bowl with water, and then rattled some of his dry food into a dish. Ignoring both, he looked up at her as she set about preparing the rest of his evening meal. She opened a tin and spooned some of the disgusting contents into his bowl.

'Here you are, Rufus. Get that down you.'

Rufus looked at it, and then away again. Heaving a deep sigh, he lay down on his blanket and closed his eyes.

'Not hungry?' she said in surprise.

She was tired herself, but not as exhausted as he seemed to be. 'See you later, then,' she said. 'Sleep well.'

8

Although she knew the paintings were out for sale in Reception because she had arranged them there, the dazzling display still took Amy by surprise.

The afternoon sun had warmed the room, and Amy propped the door open to let in some fresh air. She brought in the noticeboard too. Only the mewing of a seagull somewhere out of sight stirred the silence. She was beginning to get used to the feeling that she was here in a forgotten place, but she would welcome Grace's voice ordering her sister to do something Belinda didn't want to do, and even be pleased to hear Phoebe's clipped tones complaining because one of Gabriel's paintings was slightly askew.

She sat down at the desk to check the phone for the last number and then dialled. She listened to the ringing tone, and wondered why there wasn't an answerphone here. It would surely be a sensible thing to have in place when running a business like Penmarrow. She would make a point of asking Ben about it when he and Selina were home again. Maybe he wasn't aware that his parents could be making good use of an invention that had been around for a long time.

'Hello? This is Amy from Penmarrow, returning your call.'

The person on the other end sounded friendly, if a little quivery. As they talked, Amy imagined a little old lady, slightly old-fashioned, with her elderly husband hovering at her side ready to offer advice. Suitable clientele for Penmarrow, she thought, as she replied to the enquiries and promised to hold their booking until they had given it further thought and she had received their deposit.

She replaced the receiver and pen-cilled in the prospective clients' name in the bookings ledger for the last week in May. Anxious suddenly, she sprang to her feet. She needed to check on Rufus.

He looked up briefly at the sound of the opening door and then lowered his head again. She gazed in dismay at the line of something nasty on the floor between the door and the blanket he used as his bed.

'Oh, poor Rufus,' she cried.

There was a pile of newspaper on a low table on the other side of the room, and she used screwed-up handfuls to clear up the worst of the mess. Then she filled a bowl she found in the utility room with warm water, added some disinfectant from the cupboard under the sink, and attacked the area with the mop. The blanket had escaped which was a relief.

Murmuring words of sympathy, she knelt down beside the dog when she had finished, and gently stroked his head.

'I'd better not leave you here on your own,' she said. 'You're in a bad way, and I'll have to do something. But what?'

The tinned food she had given him yesterday had presented no problems, so it couldn't be that, and his food today was untouched. She looked round the kitchen as if that could tell her the reason for his sudden illness, but there was no clue there. She couldn't risk him being sick here again, and she couldn't leave him in her caravan either. That was definitely against the rules.

She got to her feet. 'You'll have to come with me, my poor Rufus. I'll get you back to Reception and hide you away in there while I think of what to do.'

But he didn't want to move, and whined a little more as she tried to encourage him. When at last he was on his feet, he looked as if the merest breath of wind would blow him away. He was trembling by the time she got him to Reception and she had half-carried him up the steps.

Something was definitely wrong. She looked helplessly at the telephone. It was now after six-thirty, and all sensible vets would be at home. Maybe they had emergency numbers, though. She didn't know. She didn't know either whether she should wait for a while to see if Rufus' sickness passed.

She drummed her fingers along the desk, trying to decide.

The phone rang. She picked up the receiver eagerly. It was Stella she needed now: Stella who knew about dogs, who had worked for a time helping at a local vet's. But of course it wasn't Stella. Why should it be?

'Mark?' she said uncertainly.

He sounded full of himself.

'I'm staying on here on my own, Amy,' he said. 'You can join me as soon as you like. Terry and Pete have gone back, and I'm going to have a bit of a holiday. They'll be down again next weekend, but I'm here and I need you. When can you come?'

She couldn't, of course, but it was plain he wasn't going to take no for an answer.

'I can't,' she said. 'I want to, Mark, but I can't. Not till the weekend. Oh

112

Mark, I'm so worried about Selina and Ben's dog. He's been sick. He's ill and I don't know what to do.'

'It's great here now the weather's changed, and it's going to be good again tomorrow. You can't think how brilliant it is here on Brouma.'

'I'm glad for you, Mark. Really, I am.' She gulped, nearly in tears.

'Sounds like it.'

She heard the sound of a vehicle outside, closely followed by another, and the sound of voices.

'I'll talk to you later, Mark,' she said, suddenly desperate. All she could think of now was Rufus trembling at her feet.

There was nothing for it, Amy thought a short time later. She would have to phone Callum's mobile and ask for Stella's phone number. The Allardyce sisters, full of their long day out at Land's End, had gone chattering off to their caravan. Gabriel had made himself scarce while his sister poked her head in briefly to ask how many more paintings had sold, and then went off scowling when Amy said they were still all here.

Callum answered her phone call at once. 'Amy?'

The relief of hearing his voice was tremendous.

'I need Stella's advice but I haven't got her phone number.'

'Advice? You've got problems?'

'It's Rufus. He's ill. Stella will tell me if I'm fussing too much.'

'How ill?'

'He's been sick and he's trembling a lot.' Her voice shook and she took a deep breath to control it.

'Off his food and drink?'

'It . . . it was so sudden. He was all right on the walk back from the beach, at least nearly back.'

'What was he doing on the beach?'

'I told you. We went for a walk.'

'But what did he do?'

'He ran about and rooted among the seaweed for ages. He loved it.'

'Did he eat any of it?'

'I don't know. I didn't see. He could have.'

'He needs the vet,' said Callum, his voice sharp. 'I'll be with you immediately.'

The speed that everything happened after that was alarming. Amy had barely got Rufus outside when Callum's Land Rover pulled up. Stella was beside him. She jumped out at once and helped Amy get Rufus onto the back seat.

'We have to be quick,' she said.

'I haven't put the noticeboard out. Or locked up.'

'Never mind that now,' said Callum.

He drove rapidly out through the gates, and she could see by the grip of his hands on the wheel and his grim expression that this really was serious. The vet and his team of two were clearly expecting them, and their expressions were grave. It seemed that Rufus needed an operation immediately and he was whisked off to an inner sanctum. Amy signed the consent form with a shaking hand, and then the three of them were shown into the waiting room where a coffee machine stood against the wall.

'A hot drink is definitely in order before we head home, I think,' Callum said.

With a look from Callum, Stella propelled Amy towards the chairs. 'You're in shock. We all are.'

Amy leaned back in her chair, feeling she was in a living nightmare. Callum brought three paper cups of coffee that he placed carefully on the low table in front of them.

'It's clear that Rufus must have been eating dried seaweed,' he said. 'That's what the vet thinks, and was quick to pick up on it. You heard the nurse say they had another case recently because of the hot weather?'

No one spoke for a moment. Amy wanted to ask the outcome of the other case, but the words wouldn't come.

Stella picked up her cup and drank. 'I needed that,' she said.

Amy's hand trembled as she took a sip too.

'It sounds serious,' she whispered.

She saw Stella and Callum exchanged glances.

116

'Tell me,' she said. 'Please. I have to know.'

Callum drank the rest of his coffee without answering and she could see from his taut expression that it was as bad as she thought. Or worse.

'Please God we were in time,' said Stella fervently. 'Mr Carton's good. The best. He'll save Rufus if anyone can. He'll clear his gut of seaweed before it blocks off the blood supply to the intestines. Rufus won't have chewed properly, you see, and when the dried seaweed absorbed liquid inside him, it would have expanded.'

'Drink your coffee, Amy,' said Callum abruptly.

'I have to know,' said Amy. 'I need to know. What will happen if we didn't get here in time?'

'Just pray that we did.'

'Tell me!'

Stella took a deep breath. 'The gut would most likely rupture and release poisonous acids into his body.'

'And that would be the end?'

'That would be the end,' said Stella, her voice quivering. 'And it's my fault. I should have warned you.'

'It's mine,' said Amy. 'I knew he shouldn't be eating anything he picks up, but I didn't see. I didn't watch him closely enough.'

Callum squeezed his empty paper cup and threw it in the bin. He stood up.

'Drink up, both of you, and we'll be off.'

'Not me,' said Amy.

'You'll do no good here.'

'I need to stay.'

'It could be a long time yet. They've got my mobile number, so I can contact you at once if I need to. It's best if you sleep tonight, Amy, so be sensible. You can phone here on the landline in the morning.'

'Callum's right,' said Stella.

Amy knew he was but still she hesitated.

'Rufus'll be out cold for some while yet, I think,' said Stella. 'Please, Amy, don't make things worse.'

Stella looked so pale and worried that Amy stood up too.

'Good girl,' said Callum. 'You need to eat. We all do. We'll have to stop somewhere on the way home.'

'But I didn't lock up at Penmarrow.'

'A takeaway, then. No problem.'

* * *

To find Penmarrow so quiet felt odd to Amy after the bustle of the last few hours.

Callum parked in front of Reception and got out. They had dropped Stella off in Pentowle because she needed to get back for Toby. The outside lights weren't on here, of course. The two occupied caravans had their lights on and the curtains drawn.

'Thank you, Callum,' said Amy as she got out too, clutching her warm bundle of pasty and chips. 'I'm so grateful.'

He closed the car door and shrugged off her thanks. 'I'll come with you to check that all is well.'

She knew it was no use arguing, even though she wanted to come to terms with the happenings of the last few hours, and for that she needed solitude.

They walked to Reception.

'It looks just the same as usual,' she said.

'You'll check inside to make sure?'

'Of course.'

She ran up the steps, opened the door, and switched on the light. Blinking in surprise, she gazed at the colourful array of paintings. With all that had been happening, she had forgotten about them again.

Callum, following her in, gaped at them too.

'What's this?'

Suddenly it was all too much. She dropped her warm packet of food and covered her face with her hands, her shoulders shaking.

'Did you know they were here, Amy?'

She gulped, trying not to let her tears flow. 'Please go,' she said. 'It's all right, really.'

'It's not all right with you, Amy.' Strangely, his voice had softened.

He took a step towards her and then she was in his arms, her voice muffled as she tried to break free. But he held her tightly, and for a moment she leaned against him, grateful for the warmth of his body and the strength that seemed to flow into her.

At last, he let her go.

'You need food and rest,' he said. 'If all's in order, we'll lock up here now, and talk about this another time.'

She nodded. 'Thanks.'

He felt for the switch that controlled the outside lights.

'I'm all right now.'

She was glad of the handrail as they went down the steps past the bright flowers in the stone trough.

He accompanied her to her door, waited until she was inside, and then left. Moments later, she heard the Land Rover drive away.

9

'So why did you let him eat that stuff?' the boy said, looking up at Amy with an expression of accusation on his young face.

With her mind full of Rufus, Amy took a few moments to recognise Jason Williams as he jumped out of a small green van the next morning. She had heard the vehicle and come out of Reception to investigate. She looked down at him at the bottom of the steps.

'How did you know about Rufus?'

'Aunty Stella told me. She's gone off on the early bus. A job interview, and her car's out of it. Had a collision with something or other. Typical. I said I'd drive her, but she wouldn't have it.'

'I didn't *let* Rufus eat seaweed, I didn't know he was doing it. He's never tried to eat anything he shouldn't before.'

Jason grinned. 'He was a good dog.

Friendly. I liked him.'

'You said *was*.'

'Did I? Same thing.'

'Of course it's not.' Amy caught hold of the handrail to steady herself. She had phoned earlier and been told that Rufus was sleeping soundly, that the operation had been, hopefully, in time, but they would keep him in another night for observation.

'All right then,' Jason said as if he was conferring a great favour. 'He *is* a good dog. Is that better?'

'A lot.'

'Can I come in and see the paintings?'

'You know about those, too?'

He leapt up the steps.

'Gabriel thinks it's a waste of time exhibiting here,' he said. 'Too quiet and not enough people. He wants to find somewhere down in the village, but there isn't anywhere. Only the clubhouse at the sailing club and Callum won't have anything to do with that.'

Amy wasn't altogether surprised.

Callum seemed to specialise in preventing people doing what they wanted. She held the door open.

Jason followed her in and stood in the middle of the room, gazing about him. Then he sighed, suddenly relaxing. 'Miss Allardyce said they're amazing, but she doesn't like them either.'

'Tell me what you think?'

He looked at each one carefully once more, walking round with such an expression of concentration on his face that Amy smiled.

'So what's the verdict?'

'Yeah, Gabriel's right. They need a bigger space. They're wasted here, all crowded in like that.'

'Thank you very much.'

'The other Miss Allardyce paints. Did you know that? Why not get rid of some of these and have hers here too? They'd set each other off a treat. Yeah, that's what I'd do.'

'You seem to know a lot about it.'

'Course I do. See a lot about everything as I get about, don't I? Keep my eyes open, I do.'

'So why are you here now?'

'I'm taking orders. Miss Allardyce wants a couple of pasties delivered every day whether they're here or not, so I'll leave the van outside here now till I check on that. She said I could leave them with you.'

'You can bring one of your pasties for me every day too. Could you deliver bread and milk as well if I phone through an order each day?'

'Yeah, okay. And don't worry about your dog. Aunty Stella said to tell you that, and she'll phone you later. She might call in.'

And he was off.

His cheerful presence had been a tonic, and Amy sat down at the desk feeling that there was a ray of hope now that hadn't been there before. Rufus had had his operation. All she had to do was to be patient, and get through the next couple of days without dwelling on what might have been if Callum hadn't acted quickly.

The day wore on. Jason came and went surprisingly quickly for him soon after midday. At half-past, the Allardyce sisters appeared, slightly out of breath, to say that they had just got back from a walk along the cliff path to the east.

'Come in and sit down, both of you,' said Amy in concern. 'Are you sure the walk wasn't too much for you?'

She was assured it wasn't.

'I've been thinking,' she said. It wasn't exactly true, because her mind had been full of Rufus. 'We should be exhibiting some of your paintings here too, Belinda.'

'Are you sure?' Belinda looked uncertain. 'Mine are fairly wishy-washy, dear, and the others are so vibrant. Not the same thing at all.'

'Now, don't be silly, Belinda,' her sister said with some asperity. 'This is what we wanted, isn't it?'

Amy smiled. 'Will you fetch some of them as soon as you're rested?'

Belinda got up at once, with no sign of exhaustion.

'Now for it,' said Grace when she had gone. 'I'm going to enjoy this. Which canvases shall we take down?'

The room looked really good when they had finished arranging ten of Belinda's watercolours in the positions where some of Gabriel's had been. Even Phoebe must surely approve, Amy thought. With the spare paintings stored carefully in the kitchenette, any of Gabriel's that sold could be replaced at once.

They chatted happily together, but Amy's anxiety about Rufus wouldn't go away for long. Grace was so sympathetic that Amy found herself telling them of the guilt she was still feeling.

'Put that behind you,' Grace advised. 'It was inexperience, that was all, and quite understandable.'

'So why not phone again now?' said Belinda. 'We'd all like to hear how he is.'

'They'll think I'm fussing.'

'What if you are?' said Grace. 'It's

because you love him, as we all will when we get to know him better.'

'And you don't mind having a dog on site?'

'Mind?' Grace's voice quivered a little. 'It will make it up to us for the loss of poor Buster.'

'We shall grow to love him too,' Belinda agreed.

Heartened, Amy picked up the phone.

Much later, as she got ready for bed, Amy realised with a start that she hadn't thought of Mark for hours.

★   ★   ★

The weather forecast was bad. Callum sighed as he clicked off his television and got up from the breakfast table next morning. There had been signs that it would be worsening, and he thought of Amy, anxious about that chap over on the islands and how to get to him. The sky had been a brilliant pink when he looked outside earlier. Even the dark clouds forming on the horizon were tinged with orange, and he didn't like the look of the sea either.

He cleared his breakfast things and set about the business of the day, slightly different this morning because he had agreed to give his neighbour and uncle a hand with loading up his trailer before setting off for Truro. The family had been packing up for days, moving most of their belongings into their new home with the aid of the trailer they had hired for the purpose This would be one of the last loads before they moved down to the their flat above their shop in Pentowle. His day, like yesterday, would be full, and allow him no time to visit Penmarrow in spite of his urgent wish to be there.

His colleague at work was over on the Isles of Scilly this week, checking on part of the coastline on one of the outer islands, and wasn't due back until tomorrow. This meant a longer day for him than usual, keeping an eye on some volunteers who hadn't done much work for the Intertidal Discovery team so far this year. He had met some of them at the end of his stint working for the Field Studies Council, teaching Marine Ecology in Plymouth, and knew they were keen to do at least one day a week.

His plans for combining the three small cottages into one to make a larger, more spacious property were still in their infancy. As he left home, he glanced back at the three of them, imagining how it would all look if Stella managed to achieve her ambition and moved away. It was good to have a dream, even if it might be some time before it came to fruition.

He thought of Amy again, of her struggle to cope with the shock of Rufus' sudden collapse and subsequent treatment. He wished he could have been with her yesterday, lending support.

He was still thinking of this when he arrived in the office in Truro, and for a moment, when the phone on his desk rang, he assumed that there was some sort of connection. Nonsense, of course. A daily report from the Isles of Scilly was to be expected, after all.

'How's it going then, Mike?' he asked.

'The rain's already here and the wind strengthening,' he was told. 'It's going to be worse at the weekend.'

'So I hear.'

'I'm booked on the flight to Land's End tomorrow. Can someone pick me up from there?'

'Right,' said Callum. 'Just give me the time.'

He glanced out the window. There was one more thing.

'Before you go, Mike. Any news of those photographers you saw the other day working near Brouma?'

'No sign of them, but I wasn't out in the boat yesterday. I'll keep an eye open.'

'If you would.'

Deep in thought, Callum finished the call. They might not still be over there, of course. Amy would be able to tell him. By now, she would be in constant contact with her fellow, who would be concerned about the dog, too.

★   ★   ★

How could it be, Amy wondered, that her life back in Enfield seemed to have faded into insignificance so soon? Now it was the most natural thing in the world to clamber out of bed in her caravan home, throw on her jeans and T-shirt, and go through to the galley kitchen to get the kettle on for a mug of tea. If it was grey-looking outside like today, she would sit on the window seat to drink it, looking out at the other caravans where there was no movement yet. People didn't stir early at Penmarrow.

Normally, her next job was to emerge into the fresh dewy air on Rufus-duty, but not today. There would be no delighted reaction from him when he heard her key in the lock, no walk down with him through the caravans to the cliff path.

But he might be home today! This morning she was filled with optimism, and not even the first faint hint of rain on the windowpane could dampen her spirits. She pulled on her jacket and set out through the windy morning for the Penroses' house.

The food dish had not been touched, of course, since she had taken Rufus with her two evening ago. What had she been thinking of, to leave the place in this state?

She left the door wide open and opened the window. The room smelt fusty, and she wrinkled her nose as she scraped the uneaten food into the bin and lifted it outside to deal with later. Then, filling the sink with warm soapy water, she dealt with Rufus' empty dishes and wiped down the draining board. His blanket was already folded up carefully in Reception, ready for his return. And with luck, that would be this afternoon, when she would be free to drive into town and bring him back home with her.

Home? Yes, that was definitely what Penmarrow felt like now. And the village of Pentowle too, down below, where Jason's parents had their shop and where he helped make the pasties.

She walked back to Reception through the grove of trees and the car park, and saw that the back of Gabriel's van was wide open and he was lifting something inside. She wasn't sure how he would greet her today after seeing Belinda's watercolours displayed alongside his own work. He and Phoebe had said nothing about the rearrangement, but their lack of reaction had been worrying. She had explained the reason, and assured them that as soon as the next painting had sold, she would replace it with one of Gabriel's she had taken down.

'That seems all right,' Gabriel said.

His sister had shot him an angry glance. Amy could well imagine the tirade he could expect when they got themselves back to their caravan.

She felt on the defensive now,

because of Jason telling her that Gabriel considered Penmarrow as a stopgap for his work, and a very poor one at that.

Gabriel turned to her as she approached, and his smile lit up his thin face. He wasn't wearing his hat today and his flowing locks looked as if they hadn't seen a comb for at least a month.

She smiled too. 'You look busy.'

'We're off to Truro today.'

'Not the weather for working outside?'

'I suppose not,' he said. 'I don't know why we're going. It's Phoebe's idea.'

He looked round as if checking on something. "There's no knowing with my sister. But there's something I want to buy here right now. A painting.'

Taken aback, Amy stared.

'Surely not one of your own?'

'I'll show you.'

They walked together the short distance to Reception. It wasn't yet time to open up, but already the phone was ringing.

'I'll wait,' Gabriel said.

It was another booking, and a last-minute one, from someone who had been before and was eager to come again.

'I love storms,' the man said. 'If the forecast's correct, we'll be in for some good ones soon. Jones is the name, Robert Jones, and I want to come down on Saturday.'

'I'll look forward to meeting you, Mr Jones.'

Gabriel, meanwhile, had picked up one of Belinda's paintings. 'I don't know this place.' he said, bringing it to her.

She took it from him and turned it over. There was no title, and no price marked on the back either.

'The label must have fallen off,' she said. 'I'll have to find out for you.'

'Too late now,' he said. 'My sister will be here in a minute. I'll come back later. You can hide it away for me, can't you?'

With a startled look at the clock on the wall, he was off.

* ★ ★

Amy found the Allardyce sisters about to set off when she walked down to their caravan a little while later. They were going to the north coast today, Grace told her, somewhere up near Padstow, to see if the weather was better up there.

'Sometimes it's completely different,' she said. 'Trebarwith Strand. Such a lovely name, my dear, don't you think?'

Amy agreed and then explained her mission.

Belinda's strict features softened as she smiled her pleasure at one of her paintings having sold.

'I'll come along later and see which one it is,' she said.

'When we get back,' Grace promised.

'I shall be off this afternoon collecting Rufus,' Amy said, unable to keep the good news to herself.

'Oh, my dear, that's splendid. But you'll need company surely, someone to look after him on the way back to see that he's comfortable? You can't be too careful with the poor dog.'

'Then you must go with her, Grace,' said Belinda.

Grace smiled. 'Trebarwith Strand can wait till tomorrow.'

'That's very kind.'

'That's settled, then,' said Grace. 'This morning we'll stay here. Why don't you go off for a little walk by yourself, dear? We'll guard Reception for you, won't we, Belinda? The rain could stop at any minute.'

Belinda's rare smile lit up her features.

'I'd like that above all things.'

'I'll bring my knitting,' said Grace happily.

★   ★   ★

By eleven o'clock the sky was clearing, and the sunlight on the grass was beautiful as Amy made her way down through the site to the gap in the wall. And so was the heaving sea and the scudding clouds and the fresh salty air that was full of screaming seagulls. By now, she knew only too well the vagaries of the Cornish weather, and so she shouldn't have been surprised. It seemed a good omen, though, a promise that it would all be looking up here at Penmarrow, and that somehow a magic wand would be waved and everything be as striking and illuminating as the patch of sunlight on the water.

She reached the top of the steps that she knew led down to the small secluded cove she hadn't yet explored, and was glad she had stolen this short time to refresh her spirits. Suddenly she had felt the need to escape, if only for a short while, and the kindness of the Allardyce sisters was heart-warming.

The small beach was visible now, silvery golden in the strengthening sunshine. The lines of seaweed at the water's edge looked tiny compared with the masses that had been washed up on the larger beach at Pentowle. Probably the tide had taken most of it in that direction, and left this beach relatively free.

She jumped down the last two steps onto the soft sand and looked about her with interest. It was easy to recognise the view from here of the rocky promontory to her right. She wondered what Grace had done while Belinda settled herself on a nearby rock and got out her paints and brushes and set to work. The result had certainly been pleasing, and so had the others she had worked on down here.

Such a handy little cove to access from Penmarrow. Being boundaried as it was on either side by high cliffs made it a delightfully secluded little place. A perfect spot to exercise Rufus if time were limited.

Walking across the headland to the left took only a few moments. Here, Amy found a suitable rock as a place to sit for a while, and watch the waves come inexorably in and break in sheets of brilliant foam.

She thought of Callum who loved the sea, and warmth stole through her. But she shied away from that and tried to concentrate on Mark instead. But somehow this was difficult. She was worried for his safety, of course. She had promised to join him, and that was what she must do as soon as it was possible to leave Penmarrow.

For good, her heart said.

She stood up, looked towards the steps, and saw someone leaping down. Jason!

'Hi there,' he shouted cheerfully. 'Yeah, it's great down here today. You don't get high seas like this often. It's too sheltered.'

'How did you know I was down here?'

Jason shrugged. 'Easy. I saw you.'

'It can't be twelve o'clock already.'

'Yeah, near enough. I was a bit early. I've left your pasty with the old ladies.'

'Then I'd better get back.'

'No rush. There won't be anyone about.'

He was a strange boy, seeming to take everything in his stride, even if her vanishing from Penmarrow like this in the middle of the morning wasn't a normal thing to do.

'This is like a private beach,' she said.

'As good as. No one ever comes here.'

'Except the Allardyce sisters. And me. And now you.'

He shrugged again.

'I'm on a mission from Callum.'

'Callum?'

'Yeah, he was worried. He sounded it anyway when he phoned. He got me on my mobile before I got here. He said to check on you when I called in on my rounds, just in case.'

'In case of what?'

'How should I know? He said to tell you the vet got in touch with him. They'd tried to contact you, but you weren't there. Callum knew you ought to be around somewhere.'

This was sounding bad.

'What did the vet want?'

'Nothing much, just a reminder about your dog's check-up this afternoon before he's let out: they've put the time back a bit. Four o'clock. I'll phone Callum in a bit and say you're fine.'

'Thank you,' said Amy humbly.

'See you around.' Jason was off at once, running up the steps two at a time.

Amy sat down on her rock again for a few restorative minutes. She felt stronger now, and able to cope with anything thrown at her. Anything, that is, except Callum's concern when she expected censure.

10

Stella called in briefly during late evening to ask after Rufus, and it was good to see her. She had expected a visit from Gabriel before now, to claim the painting he was keen to purchase. Their day in Truro must have proved more interesting than he had foreseen.

'So, how's the patient?' Stella asked. She was wearing a grey cashmere jersey the colour of her hair that was smoothed down in a softer way than usual. The style suited her.

'You look nice,' said Amy. 'Rufus is doing quite well, thanks. I've been feeding him small amounts at a time as the instructions said.'

'And he's keeping it down?'

'So far.'

'Good girl.' Stella smiled rather wearily, and then yawned. 'I'll leave the visiting till tomorrow if you don't mind. I'm exhausted.'

'How was your new job?'

'Hard. Too much travelling. I'll get used to it, I expect. Has Callum looked in?'

'I haven't seen him.'

'That's odd. He's not at home. Anyway, I'm glad Rufus is recovering. He'll soon be leading you a rare old dance.'

Amy smiled. 'The Penroses will be back on Friday, quite late, I think.'

'So you'll soon be off?'

'It looks like it, but I'm not sure when.' She wasn't certain either if it was fair on Jim and Maria to leave poor Rufus with them in the condition he was now in.

'Eight-fifteen?' she had said, dismayed, on phoning the *Scillonian* booking office earlier.

'For this coming Saturday only,' she was told. 'Owing to the state of the tide at Penzance.'

This put a different slant on things. It meant leaving here very early, and if Jim and Maria didn't arrive until the early hours on Saturday, it might be a problem.

Stella left soon after that. For a while, Amy sat and watched Rufus' even breathing, and wondered where Callum was that he was so late back. It had taken several attempts to get through to Mark earlier, too.

'I'm on my way back from Hugh Town,' he had said at last. 'It's great. There's a good sea running. You're not going to starve when you come, Amy, even if it's too rough for us to get off Brouma.'

But if it was too rough to get off Brouma, how was she to get there? It seemed that Mark hadn't thought of that.

'Couldn't you find somewhere to camp on St Mary's instead?' she said.

He laughed. 'You're not thinking of letting us down again?'

'Of course not.' She bit her lip.

'You'd better not. We don't take much notice of the weather forecast here. It's another world.'

'So you're managing to do some filming on your own, then?'

'More or less.' She heard the hesitation in his voice but didn't pursue it. Her thoughts were still on Rufus, and the problem he was becoming through no fault of his own. On the other end of the phone she heard engine noise fade, then a roar.

'Mark, are you all right?'

'Just a blip. It does that sometimes.'

'It's getting dark,' she said.

'I've got lights if I need them.'

'Take care, Mark.'

'See you!'

He clicked off his phone, and for a moment the resulting silence rang in her ears. She sat there thinking about Mark's work, hoping he was getting the shots of the wildlife he wanted.

The phone rang again, and this time it was Callum. She sat forward in her seat to speak to him.

'Something turned up, or I'd have got back earlier,' he said. 'Stella told me how well Rufus is doing, but I had hoped to take a look at him myself.'

'It's such a relief to have him home. I'm staying late in Reception to be with him.'

'He's not settled in your caravan?'

'It's the rules, remember?'

'I'll take full responsibility. Leave him where he is until I get there.'

Ten minutes later, she heard Callum's vehicle and went down the steps to meet him. His expression was grave as he looked down at the dog.

'Poor old boy,' Callum said, kneeling down beside him. 'You'd be happier nearer Amy tonight, wouldn't you?'

'I'd be a lot happier too,' she said.

He looked up at her for a silent moment and then got to his feet, brushing down the knees of his jeans.

Between them, they got Rufus out of the door, Callum taking his full weight once they were through and Amy following with the blanket and water bowl.

'Happier now?' Callum said when at last they had settled him in the caravan.

'Definitely,' said Amy. 'I think that's what Rufus would say, too, if he could talk to us. I could do with a coffee after all that. How about you?'

'Great.'

'How do you like it?'

'Black, no sugar.'

She smiled. 'That's easy enough.'

He smiled too as he sat down on the window-seat and stretched his long legs out in front of him.

'It's good to relax.'

'A busy day?'

'You could say that.'

He looked tired, she thought, as she made the coffee and reached inside the cupboard for a packet of chocolate biscuits. She clattered them out onto a plate and put it down on the table in front of him.

'This has been a bad time for you, Amy,' he said as she sat down opposite him with the mugs.

'Busy,' she acknowledged. 'Worrying, too, at times.'

'You've coped well. Jim and Maria

will be pleased.'

She flushed at the unexpected praise. 'I've done my best.'

He reached for his mug and held it in both hands.

'You've had little or no let-up from the responsibility of this place when everything's new to you. And then this business with poor Rufus. You need to get away from here for a while.' He looked at her gravely, and the concern she saw in his eyes was nearly her undoing.

'Yes, well. It can't be helped.'

She picked up a teaspoon and concentrated on stirring her coffee, although there was no need. He took a biscuit, looked at it for a moment, and then ate it quickly.

'An hour or two away wouldn't hurt, especially if the Allardyce sisters are happy to look after Rufus,' he said. 'I'm off to the north coast tomorrow, a lovely wild area north of Newquay. So different from here in the south. I need to check on some work being done there. It'll only take a couple of hours, but it will give you a chance to see another part of Cornwall. Why not come too?'

She twisted her hands together in her lap. An afternoon away from Penmarrow in Callum's company? The offer was tempting. She was silent for so long that he moved a little in his seat, and she felt his eyes on her with that intentness she had come to expect.

'I don't know . . . ' she began, then looked up and saw a flicker of pain cross his face.

'I see.' He put his mug down and made as if to stand up.

'No, don't go,' she said hurriedly. 'I was thinking, that's all.'

The invitation would be churlish to refuse, even if she was doubtful of the wisdom of accepting.

'Thank you,' she said. 'I'd like to come with you.'

He smiled his pleasure.

'I'll pick you up soon after two. We'll head for Bedruthen Steps first, for you to see what it's like there. I think you'll like it. Then we'll head further up the coast to Trebarwith Sands. It will be good to show you a little more of the county.'

He downed the rest of his coffee and then got up to check on Rufus before leaving. He knelt at the dog's side and Amy looked down at him, her heart full. Common sense told her that his invitation was merely a friendly gesture, that was all, because he was a considerate man; but she couldn't help a twinge of something else that she shouldn't be feeling.

★   ★   ★

Next morning, she made sure that she was busy, and that wasn't difficult because she wanted to have everything in good order for the Penroses' return. With luck, it would stop her dwelling too much on things that she didn't want to think about.

Rufus' exercise could only be taken

close to her caravan for the time being, and then for only short periods, time-consuming but necessary. At last she was able to get him, very slowly and with frequent stops, to Reception. He struggled a little as she carried him up the steps, but by the time Gabriel came he was settled on his blanket behind the desk.

Today, Gabriel was looking a little furtive.

'The painting?' he said in his gruff voice. 'That watercolour. I want another look at it.'

He was going to change his mind! In an instant, Amy thought of the vulnerable Belinda's disappointment, and how she would break the news to her.

'Of course,' she said. 'It's quite safe.'

She brought it in from the kitchenette and handed it to him.

'Have you been to that place, Dodman Head, Mr Ward . . . Gabriel?'

'I've not seen it in quite this way before.'

'Belinda's vision.'

'Quite. Can I take it with me?'

'Not until it's paid for. It's the rule,' Amy said. Her own, of course, but she had decided on this policy and was going to stick to it. All sorts of future problems might crop up if she didn't.

He handed the painting back to her. 'I shall settle up in due course.'

She smiled her relief. With a man like Gabriel, you could never be sure how he would react to anything. He seemed happy with the modest price Belinda was asking, so there was no problem there.

That came later, when Phoebe came storming in ahead of her brother, just as Amy was in the kitchenette filling his water bowl for Rufus.

She emerged in alarm at the unexpected noise. 'Phoebe!'

The colour drained from Phoebe's face, and she stared at Rufus in horror.

'You don't like dogs?' said Amy.

'What's he doing here?' Phoebe's voice was sharp as she edged away.

Amy placed the bowl near Rufus'

makeshift bed. 'He's recuperating from an operation. He won't be in here for long.'

'He'd better not be.'

'My sister's allergic to dogs,' Gabriel explained.

She shot him a venomous glance and turned to glare at Amy.

'So what happened to your promise?'

'Promise? I don't understand.'

'Or choose not to.'

Gabriel frowned. 'Leave it, Phoebe It's not important.'

'Of course it's important. You must fight for your rights, or I will.'

She glared at her brother, who hesitated for a moment and then left hurriedly, looking alarmed.

'I think you'd better explain, Phoebe,' Amy said when he had gone.

Phoebe swung round.

'I insist you display Gabriel's latest work to replace the one he bought, as you said you would. I shall bring a replacement, so just see to it.'

Amy sank down on her chair as

Phoebe stormed out. She remembered now that she had said that as soon as a painting sold, she would replace it with one of Gabriel's. What a fool she had been not to stipulate that each artist was free to replace sold ones with others of their own. Just a slight slip, and Phoebe was on her like a tornado.

She would have to move the paintings up a little to make room for this latest one of Gabriel's. On the other hand, she could utilise a book rest she had found in the kitchenette. She made sure she had it out and in position on the desk in time for Phoebe's return with a painting that she carried before her like a shield.

Phoebe, expressionless, deposited it in position.

'It's in a prime place,' Amy pointed out.

'If you say so.'

'I do say so. And in future, each artist makes a replacement on the sale of their own work. Gabriel's spare work is already stored here, so I shall do it in his case. Is that clear?'

A sniff was Phoebe's only answer, and Amy had to be content with that.

* * *

At Bedruthen Steps, the tide was halfway in, and Amy and Callum descended the steep steps to the beach. The drive from Penmarrow from the south coast to the bleaker north had interested Amy because they came through what had once been the clay country. Callum, knowledgeable about the decline of the Cornish clay industry, had pointed out the green hills that once had been white against the sky, but had been now been grassed over so they no longer looked like mountains of the moon.

'They used to show up for miles around,' he said.

'So what were they?'

'The waste matter from the clay pits. Sand burrows, they were called, other-wise known as the Cornish Alps. Only one fifth of what they got out was useable, you see. The clay industry was a huge concern, employing thousands one way and another.'

'And now it's gone.'

'But not forgotten. There's a museum, a fascinating place. And the Eden Project owes its existence to the industry, as it's in a former china clay pit.'

'It's a sobering thought how things change,' Amy said. 'It's hardly believable now.'

She thought of it again as they reached the bottom of the steps. Down here on the soft sand, they were comparatively sheltered from the wind, and she looked at the pinnacles of rock formations in surprise.

'Impressive, don't you think?' said Callum. 'Here's something that hasn't changed for hundreds of years,'

'They look as if a giant's plucked then from somewhere and just set them down here.'

He laughed. 'An apt description. Shall we walk on for a little way?'

The harder, wetter sand was easier to walk on, but as they went closer to the enormous rocks, they met the wind. Amy could see that the line of sea was getting closer, too.

'Does it always come in this quickly?' she said.

'It does here, but don't worry. We'll take a quick look, and then retire in good time.'

'So what is it you've come to check further up the coast?' she asked when they were nearly back at the steps again.

He paused. 'Some volunteer workers helping with a project we've set up to create an intertidal map. An excuse for an afternoon off, really.'

'No wonder you enjoy your job as much as Stella says you do.'

He grinned at her and indicated that she should go first up the steps. Behind them, the water was getting closer to the cliffs, and she could hardly believe that it had happened in so short a time.

'It must be a special place for tides,' she said. 'It feels eerie.'

And so it did. She shivered, and was glad when they reached the top, even though the wind was stronger now than when they'd arrived.

'What is your job, exactly?' she said as they stood still to regain their breath.

'Intertidal Discovery Project Officer,' he said.

They were walking towards Callum's vehicle now, and she could tell that he was eager to get moving. He opened the passenger door for her, and she got in quickly and fastened her seatbelt.

'That's impressive, too. What do you actually do?'

'I plan and lead field surveys, among other things. And conduct data analysis. We're mapping the habitat along the north Cornwall coastline for over two hundred miles. It's the first time it's been done in Cornwall. We record the different types of habitat, mainly between highest and lowest tides known as the intertidal area.'

'And what do you find?'

'There are hundreds of species, from

small squat lobsters to seals and the rare honeycomb worm, in a diversity of habitats.'

'So you're in charge of these volunteers too?' she said as they set off.

'It's one of my jobs to co-ordinate them. I like to visit their working area when I can. They're all keen, of course. They know their value in helping create a valuable resource to protect the habitats for future generations.'

'It sounds worthwhile.'

'I like it. It involves a lot of travelling around the Cornish coast, of course. I came back to live in Pentowle when my mother died, and I had the chance to move on from eight years working for the Field Studies Council teaching Marine Ecology. Many of the volunteers come from there. And you, Amy? What do you do when you're not running a caravan site?'

Her own job sounded boring in comparison to his, but she did her best to make it sound interesting.

' . . . and I sometimes work part-time

in an art gallery,' she concluded. 'That's what I really like.'

'So you're knowledgeable about art?'

'I'm learning.'

'And where does your photographer friend fit in?'

She hesitated. She hadn't thought of Mark for hours, and wasn't sure she wanted to talk about him now. The afternoon seemed to have dulled at the mention of his name, and Callum was frowning.

'He's neither an estate agent nor a gallery employee,' she said. 'Or anything else at the moment, apart from trying to make a career in photography.'

The sky had been pure blue when they set out from Penmarrow with the afternoon before them, but now something had happened with the covering of cloud, and she wasn't sure what. Perhaps it was the intruding thought that in two days' time she would have left all this behind her.

As they travelled up the coast, Callum told her more of what his job entailed, and then they were at Trebarwith Strand and he was engrossed with what he had come here to do. Their short time alone together was over.

Perhaps he was feeling it too, the end of a carefree hour or two. In any case, the drive home was largely silent, Callum preoccupied with his own thoughts while Amy tried to concentrate on Mark and the life he had chosen for himself.

'Thank you, Callum, for everything,' she said when they reached Penmarrow and he drove up to Reception. It sounded like a farewell, and she supposed that, in a way, it was.

She bent to stroke Rufus when Callum had gone, knowing an emptiness of mind and heart that shook her in its intensity. Her exhaustion was getting to her in a big way.

11

Amy lay in bed the next morning, gazing up at the ceiling of the caravan that almost seemed to shudder in the occasional gusts of strong wind that made the glass in the windows rattle. It was early yet, and there was no need to move, but she felt she must get up and savour every moment of what could be her last day at Penmarrow.

Rufus gave a whimper when she emerged, yawning, from her bedroom. His walk this morning was slightly longer than yesterday's, in spite of the wind. She brought him back to the caravan for a small meal, and then made her mug of tea and sat curled up on the window-seat to drink it.

The trees behind the caravans opposite were swaying, and she looked at them with interest, aware of the changing patterns the branches made against the grey sky. This new way of seeing was because of Gabriel's vision, she thought. She could now appreciate the beauty in things that had never occurred to her before. And it was his vision that had done this for her.

She wished Stella were here now so they could talk about it. They had had some good discussions, she and Stella. But dwelling on that was not going to help her. Her first job this morning was to check that the carton of milk in the fridge in the house was still within the use-by date. This was quickly done, but Amy decided she would get some more anyway, with a few other necessities.

During the morning, she took Rufus to the house where Jim and Maria would expect to find him.

'I hope this feels like home to you now,' she told him.

A quick phone call to Mark when she returned to Reception? Why not? No surprise when it went straight to voicemail, but it had been worth a try.

She was glad that Grace Allardyce

was with her as she drove Rufus into town for his check-up. The strong wind made her uneasy, and she could sense Rufus didn't like it, either. Grace talked to him soothingly, promising some nice little dog biscuits when they arrived.

All was well, and all Rufus needed now, apart from care with his feeding, was someone to watch him carefully on his frequent short walks.

Belinda emerged from the kitchenette with a duster in her hand when Amy and Grace arrived after settling Rufus at the house.

'That nice Mr Ward came to pay for my painting,' she said. Her cheeks had a faint tinge of pink in them. 'I've got the money here.' She plunged her hand deep into the pocket of her skirt and pulled out three ten-pound notes. 'Can you believe he paid all this money for my little effort?'

'Easily,' said Amy, smiling at her. 'I hope it will be the first of many sales. You deserve it.'

Belinda looked down at the notes in

her hand, obviously overcome.

'Twenty-five percent of it goes to Amy, dear,' Grace reminded her.

'Oh yes, of course. Silly me.' Belinda thrust the notes into Amy's hand. Her lips were moving as she worked out the money she would receive.

'I'm going back to the house now to give him his tea,' Amy said. 'Would you mind staying here just a little longer?'

There was no need really, because it was normally her time off, but she could see how much Belinda and Grace were enjoying themselves.

★   ★   ★

Callum was home earlier than usual on Friday afternoon because the meeting in Truro had ended soon after four. Mike, his assistant, had a chance over lunch to fill him in on more detail of the key areas for intertidal habitats on Scilly.

'Marine Conservation Zones on some of the inhabited islands,' Mike had said, as if no one had thought of that before.

'Lately, there's been a lot of evidence of visitors landing where they used not to. Litter's been found, and remains of barbecue fires. The trouble is, there's so much coastline.'

'The hundred thousand visitors to Scilly per year have to go somewhere.'

'That many?'

'Near enough.'

Mike paused in the act of wiping his mouth after he had downed the last of his beer. 'But not all on the same island, of course, or all the same time. You're not advocating that sort of carry-on, I hope?'

'Why not? Everyone encouraged to congregate on one particular island to leave the others pollution-free for all to enjoy. But of course they wouldn't be able to, would they, because they'd all be holed up together in one place . . . '

Mike stared at him in astonishment. 'You don't mean it?'

Callum grinned. It was so easy to wind Mike up, and sometimes it was hard to resist.

'All right, you win,' Mike said, smiling too. 'What's got into you today, anyway?'

Callum had wondered that himself. There was a lot on his mind at the moment: concern for the Penroses, and what was to become of Penmarrow, being one particular worry. Of late, Jim and Maria's interest had obviously not been in it, and that had shown in many small ways. It seemed that this season would be as bad as the last, when even in high summer there were more vacancies than occupancies.

There was Stella to consider too, and his own plans to convert the cottages into a single more convenient unit would have to be postponed yet again. The only sensible thing was to let the vacant cottage for the time being. He had contacted Harmer and King, reputed to be the best estate agents in town, who had already come to take details to put on their website. They had set up an appointment to view already for later this afternoon, but he wasn't too sure about having the Wards in close proximity, should they decide to take it.

Callum indicated Mike's empty glass. 'Another?'

'Not for me,' Mike had said, scraping back his chair as he stood up. 'I must get off.'

'Before you go ... Any sighting of people on the smaller islands? Brouma, for instance?'

'That wasn't my brief, was it, that sort of detective work? You're not really serious about one of the islands being set up?'

'I take it that's a no?'

'Too windy to venture far on my last day. And it's getting worse, by all accounts.' Mike nodded at the window. 'You only have to look out there.'

Already the trees were bending about like frantic beings, although not quite as badly as earlier. With luck, the strong winds would be blowing themselves out soon.

'See you on Monday, then,' Callum

said as he got up and shrugged his arms into his jacket.

As Callum walked up the steep path to his front door, he wished he had asked Mike more about the visitors he had encountered on dry land, especially those wielding cameras and other photographic equipment.

He was aware that young Jason was prowling about the empty cottage next door, no doubt checking that everything had been cleared out. The boy came out of the cottage and banged shut the door behind him.

'What are you up to then, Jason?' Callum called as he slotted the key in his lock.

'Just lookering.'

The use of the old word told Callum a great deal. Jason had always disliked change until he had got used to it, and the moving of the family down to Pentowle most of all.

'Coming in for a bit?' he said.

Jason appeared behind him in seconds. 'Lead the way.'

'Scrounging for food, are you? Or looking for buried treasure?'

'Yeah, something like that.'

Callum plugged in the kettle. 'There's a packet of fig bars in the tin. Help yourself.'

'Want one too?'

Callum shook his head as he took off his jacket and threw it over the back of a chair. 'I'm expecting visitors soon. They want to take a look at the place next door, your old place.'

'They want to live there?'

'Apparently, they've been looking for somewhere suitable for the last day or two, and they think this might be it.'

'It'll be suitable, all right,' Jason said glumly. 'Just you wait and see.'

'What's your new place like?'

'Don't you know?'

'Of course I know, but I want to know your reaction.'

'It's handy for the village.'

'Right in the centre of it,' Callum agreed.

'Not far to go to work.'

'That's true.'

'It's all right, I suppose. Mum likes it. But I like a bit of space. See a few miles. Yeah, that's me.'

Callum laughed. 'You've always been a bit of an oddbod, haven't you, Jason? You can always come up here to look at the view.'

'That Gabriel chap's been hanging round painting. He wants somewhere in Pentowle to show his work.'

With a jolt of comprehension, Callum thought of the canvases in bright colours he had glimpsed when he was at Penmarrow last. He should do something about that before Jim arrived and got the shock of his life.

'I won't ask what you think of his work, Jason,' he said.

Jason shrugged and reached for another fig bar. 'I don't like the thought of the old place next door getting smeared up with paint.'

'Any reason why it should?'

'When are they coming?'

Callum glanced at his watch. 'Who?'

'Old Gabriel and that potty sister of his?'

'What's potty about her?'

'You'll find out if you let them come to live here.'

'Why should you assume they are the viewers?'

'It's obvious.'

'Not to me, it isn't.

'It is to Mum and Dad.'

'How about your Aunty Stella?'

'Her too.'

Callum frowned. The thought of a family committee picking up on aspects of his life and commenting on them was unnerving.

'Yeah, thin end of the wedge, Dad said.'

Callum was startled. 'What d'you mean?'

Jason said nothing, but Callum saw the look of deep wisdom in the boy's eyes, and remembered Phoebe's startled surprise on meeting him in Truro on Wednesday. He had thought then that it didn't seem quite genuine, but had then dismissed it as unworthy. She had been her old charming self, and he had enjoyed their brief lunch together, but there had been an edge to her voice he had found disturbing. He had put this down to the awkwardness of meeting again after some time, but could there be a deeper reason? There was her gatecrashing of the prize-giving at the sailing club on Sunday, too. She hadn't stayed long. 'Just come to make contact,' she had said above the noise at the bar.

He had assumed she was here on holiday with friends, but when had Phoebe ever had friends? Certainly not when they had known each other.

Jason took the last of the biscuits and then rattled the wrapping to check for the odd crumb. Then he crumpled it and threw it in the small bin by the back door. 'I'll leave you to it, then.'

Deep in thought, Callum watched him go, and then set about making coffee for himself. He hadn't told anyone the names of the prospective new tenants, but it seemed to be public knowledge. Jason's hints had been disturbing, and he began to have serious doubts about the wisdom of letting the property to them.

He wondered how Gabriel had the effrontery to return to Pentowle after his ignominious departure. He had come off the worse in the brief encounter with his uncle — who had taken exception to the insults to himself Gabriel had bandied about — and probably still had the scar to prove it.

But showing Phoebe and her brother round would give him a breathing space before he set out for Penmarrow to check on things there.

The memory of Amy's face swept into his mind with disconcerting suddenness. He saw her expression of wonder as she viewed the stark pinnacles of rock at Bedruthen Steps, and the way her mouth turned up at the corners when she was amused at something he said. Her soft hair had fallen around her face as they met the wind on the top of the cliff, and she had shaken it back in such a charming way that he had longed to brush it back for her and kiss those lips.

She had been so patient, waiting for him to finish the checking he had come to do, as if she understood perfectly that these things must take a lot of his attention. And then he thought of her expression when she talked of this chap on Scilly — this chap who didn't deserve someone like Amy.

12

'So, how are things?' Stella asked, tapping on the open door of Amy's caravan. 'I thought I'd call in to check.'

'Stella!' Amy said with pleasure. 'Come in and shut the door before we get blown away.' She indicated the frying pan she had got down from the cupboard. 'I was just about to have a quick fry-up. Interested in joining me?'

'Yes please.'

'Mushroom omelettes coming up, with fried tomatoes and jacket potatoes from the microwave. And there's salad . . . '

'A feast,' said Stella, throwing herself down on the window-seat in the sitting area with a sigh of relief.

'Busy day?'

'You could say that. I don't know if I can stick doing this sort of thing for long, even for the money. So how is the invalid now?'

'A little stronger each day.'

'You don't sound too sure about it.'

'Oh, but I am. It's just that . . . I don't know. I'm not sure if it's fair to leave Rufus with Jim when he has such worries.'

'But he and Maria offered to look after him.'

'But not in the state Rufus is in now.'

'You can't take Rufus with you?'

Amy broke five large eggs into the mixing bowl, reached for the milk and a glass half-full of water to add to them, and attacked the mix with the hand beater. For a moment, she made no reply, and then when she had finished, said, 'He'd have to be left for hours each day. And Mark would be dead against having a dog with us. He hates animals. It would be enough to . . . '

She was afraid of how it would be, but was ashamed to admit it even to herself. She had done her best to pretend that Mark's lack of communication had been because of the long hours he was spending out in his boat;

but, deep down, she suspected there was a deeper reason.

'He hates animals?' Stella said in disbelief. 'You're joking!'

'It happens.'

'But, a wildlife photographer?'

Amy stared down at the spatula in her hand. 'I know.'

Stella was thoughtful. 'I wish I could look after Rufus for you, if you feel you have to go. Bad timing. Grace and Belinda Allardyce?'

'I can't ask them. I don't know how they would cope with him full-time.'

'Did you hear on the radio that all flights to St Mary's are cancelled for tomorrow? The *Scillonian* is still sailing, though. You're lucky you're booked on that.'

'Only provisionally. I have to be there for seven-fifteen.'

'You'll do it, if you have to.'

'I suppose so.' Amy flicked the second omelette over.

'Well, let's enjoy the meal,' said Stella briskly.

Amy slipped the omelettes and tomatoes onto two plates, removed the potatoes from the microwave, and produced the bowl of salad from the fridge.

They ate in silence. When Amy got up to make coffee, Stella stirred a little in her seat and said, 'It's going to seem strange here without you, Amy. You'll come back and see us?'

Amy hesitated. She hadn't thought that far ahead. Would Mark want to come down to Pentowle when he was so busy striving to make a success of his new career?

'I hope so,' she said.

'But what will happen about Rufus?'

'Selina and Ben are going to pick him up the day after they get home. That was the arrangement.'

'And that's when?'

'Monday week.'

'You're looking solemn,' said Stella.

Amy gave a little sigh. 'Perhaps.'

Stella left soon after that, promising to keep in touch whatever happened. Amy was sad to see her go.

* ★ ★

The walks had been getting a little longer each day, but Amy hadn't wanted to overdo things, even though she suspected she was being overcautious. Rufus hadn't yet managed all the way down to the cliff path. This windy evening, she walked him round to the car park and then back again. Then she sat with him on the steps to Reception in the shelter of the building to think things through. It was still only eight o'clock, and it would be hours yet before Jim and Maria put in an appearance.

She looked up suddenly, and saw Callum coming towards her from the direction of the cliff path. His jacket had blown open, and he smoothed down his ruffled auburn hair as he caught sight of her sitting there.

'Hi there, Amy.'

'Hello, Callum.'

She wondered why he hadn't driven up this windy evening as he usually did, instead of walking along the cliff from Pentowle.

'Trying to get a breath of fresh air?' he said.

She smiled as she stood up and came down the steps to meet him. 'Like you, I think. There's plenty of it about.'

'I needed to fill my lungs, and the walk was an excellent way of doing it.'

'Is anything wrong?' she asked.

She saw the lines of weariness deepen round his mouth. 'I came to check that all was well.'

She shrugged, suspecting there was another reason, too. 'I've done the best I can here,' she said.

'You know there's an earlier sailing than usual from Penzance tomorrow?' He spoke abruptly in a tone of voice she hadn't heard him use before.

'Because of the tides? I'm aware of that.'

'I assumed you must be.'

The silence between them was heavy and she didn't know what else to say.

'I'd like to see these paintings I've

been hearing about,' he said at last.

Surprised, she took a deep breath. 'Then come this way.'

Rufus got unsteadily to his feet as she unlocked the door, and he followed them inside.

'This is Gabriel Ward's work?' Callum said when they were inside.

'All except the watercolours. They're Belinda's.'

Callum nodded absently. He was staring at the canvases as if he couldn't see enough of them.

'May I?' He moved to pick one up and held it out at eye level, his expression inscrutable.

Amy waited. Dusk was beginning to fall outside, blurring the outlines of the furthest caravans.

'How much is he asking for this one?' Callum said.

'You like it?'

'He's caught the gleam of the sea between the trolley wheels to perfection. It's clever. I'd like to purchase it.'

'The price is on the back.'

Callum turned the canvas over and nodded.

'I'll take it.'

'I'll get the cash tin.' She smiled as she produced the receipt book. This was decidedly unexpected.

'You seem to find this amusing.'

'Not really. I was prepared for a blast of disapproval, that's all.'

'Can I take it with me now?'

'Not till it's paid for.'

'Then I must leave it here until tomorrow. I came out rather hurriedly to escape a difficult situation, and left my wallet behind. I'm afraid I ran away in a decidedly cowardly fashion.'

'You, cowardly?'

'I'm gratified by your surprise.'

'I always expect the unexpected.'

'Wise girl. Then how's this for unexpected? Jim rang me just before my prospective tenants arrived. It was lucky or I might have missed his call. Did he try here? No? He wanted me to tell you myself, and it was a good excuse to cut short the viewing of the empty cottage next door to me. The Wards want to rent it but I'm not keen on having them as tenants. There was a bit of a scene. I'm afraid Phoebe is highly suspicious of my reasons. She blames you.'

'Me?'

'She thinks I'm going to rent it to you. Of course I would, gladly, if I thought there was any chance of your taking it.'

She said nothing, and he didn't seem to expect an answer. She thought of how it would be if she stayed in Pentowle a week or two longer. Definitely longer if she gave in her notice at work, something she knew would be appreciated because business was so bad. *But no, don't even think of it . . .*

'Ah, well,' he said.

'And the surprise?' she asked, suddenly remembering.

'No big deal, really. It's just that Jim and Maria are bringing his sister back with them, possibly for good. That's why they'll be very late. They want to

186

get straight here and not stop overnight on the way, and they'll need to take frequent short stops. He doesn't want you to stay up for them.'

'Very well.'

'He understands that you need to get off early tomorrow. He expects to be around to see you before you go.'

Amy glanced at Rufus, lying full length on the floor at her feet. 'I'm not sure yet what to do.'

'Have you heard from your friend over there?'

She shook her head. 'He could be out somewhere, busy filming.'

'And too busy to answer when he must know it's likely to be you and you're concerned about him?'

'I think so, yes.'

This was a dreadful confession to make, especially to Callum, who was looking as if his opinion of her was at an all-time low. She didn't blame him. Mark was relying on her joining him, and she had promised. Of course he was impatient to get on with it with no distractions, because the filming meant so much to him. It should mean a lot to her, too, for his sake.

'And you, Amy?' Callum said. 'How much does it mean to you to be over there?' The words seemed to have been wrung out of him.

'You ask me that?'

He frowned. 'I can see I don't need to.'

'No.'

'You've made your *Scillonian* booking?'

'They will hold it for me until an hour before sailing.'

'So your options are open?'

She looked at Callum without speaking.

'I've got leave owing to me,' he said, his voice strained. 'I'll take Rufus to my place and look after him there for you until your sister collects him.'

'You'd do that?' Amy said, marvelling.

'That and more, if need be.'

She stood quite still. Callum expected

her to go tomorrow. In fact, he encouraged it. He knew the value of promises made and kept, and was seeing to it that her excuses were just that. Excuses. She knew now, with sudden clarity, that that was exactly what they were.

She looked down at the floor, that seemed to be coming up to meet her in an extraordinary way, and closed her eyes for the time it took to steady herself.

'Leave Rufus here in Reception overnight,' Callum said. 'Leave the rest to me. Stella and I between us will explain everything to Jim if you don't get a chance to see him. Will that do?'

She nodded, unable to speak for the tears in her throat.

13

Amy thought she wouldn't sleep, but she must have dozed off, because she was awakened by the shaking of the caravan and the sound of the wind like mournful banshees or something worse. The sea was thunderous too. Heart thudding, she sat up and listened. The outside lights were still on, of course. Should she get up and check that all was well?

Stella had said that all flights had been cancelled, and that was disturbing. Was the wind getting worse? Having other things to think about, she hadn't had the TV on yesterday for the latest weather forecast. Now she wished she had. She hoped that Mark was safe in his tent in a sheltered place on Brouma. She had to find out, and the only way to do that at this moment, late as it was, was for her to try his mobile again.

She got out of bed, pulled on her jeans and jacket, thrust her feet into trainers, and pulled open the door that was nearly wrenched out of her hand. Head down, she made for Reception.

Rufus blinked sleepily at her when she switched on the light.

'It's all right, boy,' she said. 'Go back to sleep. It's the middle of the night.'

She hoped it was all right, but there was no reply when she heard the ringing tone miles away on Mark's deserted island. It cut out and went to voicemail. She left a message and then stood, breathing deeply.

'Don't panic,' she muttered.

But in the early hours of the morning, it was hard not to.

Rufus stirred slightly, his tail beginning to move. She smiled as she bent to stroke him. There were good reasons for Mark not to be answering his phone. He could be in a deep sleep; he might had left his phone elsewhere and it was ringing with no one to hear it; or he was snug in his sleeping bag and couldn't be bothered to move. Anything, even his battery being down. But none of the reasons entirely convinced her.

Now she became aware of a car engine above the sound of the wind, and ran to the door in time to see a vehicle drive towards the car park, stop, reverse and come to a stop in front of Reception. For a wild moment, she thought it was Callum; then saw that the vehicle wasn't a Land Rover but a small saloon.

Jim? She knew it must be, and could see she was right when his figure emerged from the vehicle holding a walking stick. He looked up at her standing at the top of the steps, and she ran down to join him. In the harsh electric light he looked years older that when she had last seen him.

'Amy, my dear!'

'I'm so glad to see you, Jim. A long journey. I thought you might have gone straight to the house.'

'I would have done if I hadn't seen the light in this building.'

'I came to make a phone call.'

He glanced at his watch. 'An emergency?'

'Yes, no. I hope not.'

'But at this time of night?'

'I needed to know something, but I didn't get an answer. I have to go straight away in the morning, you see. And there are the paintings in there. I forgot to tell you and . . .'

She broke off, knowing she wasn't making sense, but she couldn't burden him with anything else at this time. 'I'm so sorry. I have to go. Here's the key.'

'Thank you, my dear. Of course you must go. But it's nearly morning now.'

At once she was contrite.

'I'm sorry to keep you. Please . . .' She glanced inside the car at his sleeping passengers. 'Is there anything I can do for you?'

'No, my dear, go back to bed. We'll talk before you leave.'

'Callum is going to look after Rufus and explain things. That's why we've left Rufus in Reception for tonight.

He's got the spare key.'

'Go, my dear. And have a good journey tomorrow. Thank you for all you've done here. I don't know how we can thank you.'

'No, please, I . . . '

'If you need a bed on your return journey, you know where to come.'

There was little to say after that. Jim, Maria and his sister had arrived safely. She would be leaving Penmarrow in good hands.

★   ★   ★

The wind was still rattling the caravan when Amy lifted her luggage down the steps and headed for the car park. The dark sky was already beginning to lighten in the east. It occurred to her with a pang of dismay that she hadn't said farewell to the Allardyce sisters. She should have thought of it, but it was too late now. She would write to them and explain.

Now, reaching her car, she stood still

to take her last breath of windy Penmarrow air, and to listen to the sea roaring in the distance.

At a sound behind her, Amy swung round. For a moment, she thought it was Jim, but instead she saw Phoebe Ward advancing on her through the dim light with an expression that boded no good. Her loose cloak swung round her, and she pulled it to her tightly.

'What do you think you're doing?' Phoebe hissed.

Amy hesitated.

Gabriel, laden with a bulging bag with several large paint brushes protruding from it, joined them. He dropped the lot to the ground and the bag, bursting open, shed some of its cargo of sketchbooks.

'We know what your game is,' Phoebe accused.

Amy stared in dismay. This was a nightmare, and she would wake in a minute and find herself back in the caravan, panicking because she had left it too late to get to Penzance. But she wasn't in the caravan, and the panic was getting worse.

'What do you mean?'

'Don't play the innocent with me. Creeping out to him, thinking no one would notice. But we saw your lights go on. We knew what you were doing.'

'Let her speak for herself,' said Gabriel, pushing his windblown hair away from his face as he shuffled to his feet.

'After what she's done, making sure he didn't rent the place to us because she had other plans? You saw his reaction yesterday when we showed up. You saw the way he clammed up when I demanded to know who his new tenants were.'

'This is ridiculous,' Amy said.

'So where are you going at this early hour?' Gabriel asked the question as if he really wanted to know.

'I told you,' Phoebe said furiously.

'I have to be at Penzance for the *Scillonian* sailing today,' said Amy. 'I'm cutting it fine. I'm late.'

Her luggage was still on the ground at her feet, and she heaved it up now and put it in the car. She shut the lid with a resounding bang, not caring who heard. She didn't deserve this, and there was no good reason to put up with it a moment longer. Penmarrow was no longer her responsibility, and neither were its clients.

'What?' Phoebe's scornful laugh filled the air. 'Late? You don't expect us to believe that? Don't you know there's no sailing of the *Scillonian* today?'

'I expect nothing,' said Amy with a firmness that was increasingly hard to maintain.

'We're off for good, and we want Gabriel's paintings. All of them. Now.'

'I can't help you there. I no longer have the key.'

But Phoebe was having none of that. She stepped forward, but Amy was too quick for her. She was inside her car with her engine running, anxious to get right away with as much speed as she could.

She slowed down as she approached Pentowle. Early as it was, there was movement outside the village shop, and she saw that Jason had the door open and was retrieving some bins that had been blown across the pavement. He saw her and waved, and her spirits felt lighter because of it.

She stopped the car and wound down the window. He was with her in seconds.

'I need to cancel my daily pasty, and I forgot to tell you.'

'Yeah. Okay.'

'I'm a bit late. I got held up by Gabriel Ward and his sister.'

'You'll make it,' he said. 'If the *Scillonian*'s still sailing, that is.'

'It either is or it isn't, and I'm going down there to find out.'

And she was off. She could feel the wind buffeting the car. It would be worse over on the islands, but she wouldn't think of that.

She was well on her way now, travelling past Truro with the view of the cathedral on her right in the brightening sky. She leaned forward to switch on the radio, pressing buttons for the news channel, and then only half-listened to the traffic problems upcountry. The road ahead of her was clear, and she speeded down past the turning to Threemilestones, where Mark had spent childhood holidays with an aunt he still remembered fondly enough years after her death to suggest he take Amy there one day to photograph the old place. That was when they had first met and he was just getting started with his new camera. It hadn't been mentioned during the months since, not even when he knew she was coming down to Cornwall.

And now to the main part of the local news again, and travel conditions in the south-west.

Even if she hadn't believed Phoebe, the increasingly bad weather conditions should have alerted her to the possibility of the *Scillonian* being cancelled. But the announcement, when it came, took her so much by surprise that she swerved towards the bank, swerved out again, and braked. She came to a stop, thankful that the road was empty.

The Phoebe episode had obviously got to her more than she had thought, but that was no excuse. She was a liability both to herself and to other drivers, and the best thing would be to get herself off the road to somewhere quiet where she could wait until such a time as she could get food and drink this early on a Saturday morning. And she needed to be somewhere away from all these trees creaking and swaying overhead.

★   ★   ★

Jim Penrose knew that the door to Reception had been locked, because Amy had handed him the key before returning to her caravan for what was left of the night. So why was it now swinging open?

He mounted the steps, avoiding the

spilt earth from the upturned trough. A broken lock! There was trouble here.

Inside, he stopped, transfixed. The watercolours must be Belinda's work. The style was hers. But had she gone raving mad, to produce these other absurd monstrosities it hurt his eyes to look at?

He averted his gaze and saw the empty dog blanket behind the desk where Rufus should have been. Alarmed, he looked closer.

Amy had said that Callum was going to pick the dog up and take him to his place, but surely not at this early hour? It was odd that he hadn't taken the blanket, too. And to have left the door wide open with a broken lock? Definitely not. So in that case, it was likely that the dog had gone off somewhere, and might not be far away.

He went to the door. The sign had blown over, even although someone had wedged it against the wall behind the stone trough that was now on its side. He called the dog's name, but the sound was lost in the force of the wind, and so was his piercing whistle. He gave up and went back inside and looked down at the floor, hoping that somehow he had been mistaken and imagined the blanket there. But no, there it was, and the dog had gone.

There was nothing for it but to phone Callum, early as it was. An emergency. Callum would understand.

He placed his walking stick against the desk and pressed the button on the phone to connect with Callum's mobile, expecting to get straight through. But something was going on. Callum was unavailable to speak. Slightly thrown, Jim tried to remember the landline number and couldn't. It was some moments before he located the telephone directory, and even then his eyes wouldn't focus at first. He listened to the ringing tone for nearly five minutes before he gave up.

He stood up and leaned his weight on the desk. He was getting too old for this. Years ago, he would have scoured the site by now, and checked in both directions along the cliff path, windy as it was. He would have relied on no one but himself to solve the problems and locate the dog.

He tried the mobile again.

'Callum Savernack speaking.'

Jim could say nothing for the relief that hit him.

'Hello?'

'Callum, it's me.'

'Ah, Jim. Good to hear from you.'

'There seems to be a bit of a problem.'

'Where are you?'

'We got home to Penmarrow in the early hours. It's the dog. He's not here. Did he go with you?'

'Don't worry, Jim. Amy must have changed her mind and taken him with her.'

'The door was swinging wide open. She wouldn't leave it like that, would she, or knock over the flower trough? There's earth all over the steps.'

He could almost feel Callum's shock reverberating through the air.

'You've searched the place?'

'I've called and whistled. The dog could be anywhere.'

'I'll come at once.'

★　★　★

But Callum had something to do first, something important that would take, with luck, only a few minutes. He had hesitated about doing this before, because it might alert the authorities to this foolish chap camping illegally on an uninhabited island. But weather conditions were worsening, and he might be in serious trouble.

So, first an email, to be followed by a phone call later.

He switched on his laptop.

14

Amy had almost reached the A30 before she stopped the car again. There was little shelter from the elements here, but there were no gloomy trees with swaying branches overhead to worry her. It was as good a place as any to take stock and consider her options.

She looked at her watch. Mark might be awake now, lying in his sleeping bag and frustrated because his plans were foiled by the ferocity of the wind. She pulled out her mobile. Again there was no reply, only this strange sound that told her nothing. By now, Mark could have heard about the sailing cancellation and tried to phone her at Penmarrow. He would have to be away from Brouma to do that, of course, but perhaps he was safely on St Mary's. She must hold on to that thought.

It was far too early to expect Jim to

be in Reception. Even Rufus would still be asleep, because it was unlikely that Callum would have collected him yet. So she had a decision to make that was no decision really. She switched on the ignition and turned the car to head back the way she had come.

* * *

She drove into the car park and saw at once that the Wards' van had gone. The fierce, salty air stung her lips as she got out of the car, and the roar of the sea sounded like thunder.

Head down, she made her way to Reception, and then stopped in surprise at seeing the stone trough wedged against the door and a heap of spilt compost and the untidy heap of dead-looking primulas at the top of the steps. Immediately, she thought of the piles of red campion and cow parsley she had come across the day she arrived at Penmarrow, because Callum had been working there with his strimmer.

Or so she had thought. But these weren't wild flowers. These were cultivated ones planted by the owner of the property.

Her worry about Mark was making her light-headed.

Jim had obviously overslept. The place looked as deserted as it had on her first arriving at Penmarrow.

She stood for a moment leaning into the wind, considering. The village shop was open. She would go back there now. At the car she stood still for a moment, listening. Incredible to hear the yelp of a dog above the noise of the wind, but in a brief silence between gusts that was exactly what she heard. Rufus!

He came out of the bushes, his black body quivering and his tail wagging in delight.

'What are you doing here, Rufus? I don't believe it! You should be safe with Callum.'

This was worrying as well as mystifying. What should she do, who to ask? Jason, of course, who else?

She bundled Rufus into the car and set off for Pentowle.

'So they told you?' Jason said when he saw her. 'Yeah, they've been out looking along the cliff path, Callum and Aunty Stella.'

'But why was Rufus on the loose?'

Jason shrugged.

'No one said.'

'I found him in the Penmarrow car park.'

He brightened.

'So you've got him?'

'He's outside in my car. Why didn't Callum collect him as he promised?'

'Those two artist people, the Wards. You said they tried to stop you leaving. Yeah, what if they tried to break into the place? Callum phoned here when he found the door swinging open and your dog gone. Dad's been looking round the village. Me too. We didn't find him.' Jason picked up the telephone. 'I'll tell Callum. Mum's in the back room. Go on through. She'll make you a hot drink.'

'I've got to get back,' Amy said. 'We're expecting a client.'

'He won't be this early.'

Amy hesitated. He had a point.

'Give me your car key?' Jason said, holding out his hand for them. 'I'll bring the dog in.'

'It's not locked.' Securing the car had been the last thing on her mind.

Mrs Williams was in the room now, fussing over her just as her son said she would. The wholesome scent about her spelt warmth and comfort that was appealing, and Amy was glad to sink into a soft chair while tea was prepared and poured out.

'You'll be hungry?'

'A bit,' Amy confessed.

'More than a bit, I should think, by the look of you.'

Before she knew it Amy had a plate of buttered toast placed before her on a small table that the older woman pulled towards her with one pink-slippered foot. 'You're very kind,' she said.

'Nothing you don't deserve, I'm sure.'

'Yeah,' said Jason, coming back in to the room with Rufus. 'You'll get an extra big pasty at lunchtime.'

'Get back to your work,' his mother said crisply.

Jason grinned at Amy and left.

★ ★ ★

Callum received Jason's phone call as he and Stella met at the brow of the rising ground on the cliff path.

'All's well,' he said, clicking off his mobile. 'The dog's been found, and Amy's there at the shop.'

'We'd better get back to the house and tell Jim.'

'I'll go. I'll phone first.'

'Then I'll join the others.'

Callum nodded. 'You do that.'

He set off swiftly, thinking hard. He had got to know Jim and Maria so well over the years, first as friends of his parents, and then as his own, who were always there for him as he was getting his career together and then changing direction in midstream.

Not once had they offered a word of criticism when he had fallen for Phoebe, and their patience in letting events run their course to the inevitable end was admirable. So it was natural to have their interests at heart, even if his ideas didn't always coincide with theirs.

He had tried to insist that they took fewer bookings and conserved their energy to find the perfect property for their retirement. It had been obvious to him for some time that Jim and Maria were finding Penmarrow hard to cope with. Recently, to his relief, they were beginning to agree with him. They had made him promise to keep this to himself.

He was not at all surprised to hear that they were bringing the sister back with them for the foreseeable future, but he wasn't sure it was wise with Maria's broken wrist to contend with. Not only that, but the house was unsuitable for invalids. Jim's wan appearance as he came down the steps of the building earlier had been a shock. The strength of the wind had him clinging to the balustrade, looking as if he might be blown away at any moment. He had persuaded Jim to wait in the house with Maria while he and Stella set out along the cliff path, where he knew Amy had often taken Rufus for walks.

He found Maria in their kitchen, making tea with one hand, and he was tempted to blurt out that they should sell up immediately and move out before the place could run down even more. Of course, he couldn't do that, but something in his face must have alerted Maria to his true feelings.

'Sit down, Callum,' she said in her gentle voice. 'Jim will be back in a minute. We've been thinking . . . '

★　★　★

'You'd think I was his long-lost best friend,' Stella said as Rufus rushed at her, tail wagging.

212

'You are,' said Amy from her seat by the fire.

'Easy to see you've missed your vocation,' Jason's mother observed as she placed a fresh pot of tea on the table in front of Amy.

Stella sank down on the spare chair. 'Too true. I'd be looking after a lot of Rufuses if I had my way.' She leaned forward to help herself to tea.

'And looking after them a whole lot better than that nephew of ours.'

'It's not Callum's fault,' said Amy. 'Jason's worked out what could have happened. Sounds like Rufus leapt to the defence of Reception when someone tried to break in.'

'Don't tell me,' said Stella. 'The Wards! Barked his head off, no doubt, the brave boy.'

'They wanted Gabriel's paintings. They were just off when I left very early, and I didn't have the key. They wouldn't have known Rufus was there, and Phoebe's terrified of dogs. She could have panicked.'

Amused, Stella patted Rufus, who wriggled in delight.

'I trust the paintings are still there?' Jason's mother looked disapproving.

'They should never have been there anyway. Jason thinks there should be a proper exhibition place, like those buildings out the back at your place, Stella, that aren't suitable for dogs.'

'Jason's full of ideas, some good and some bad.'

'Accessible from the village, plenty of space to park cars. I tell him he should be running the gallery himself when it's set up, but he's not interested.'

'I should think not,' said Stella. 'More sense to concentrate on dogs.'

'You've got dogs on the brain.'

'I wish.'

The phone rang in the shop, and Jason's mother went to answer it.

Stella got up and stretched. 'I'd better get myself home, and phone through my excuses for being late for work.'

Amy looked at her in dismay.

'And Saturday's your busiest day!'

'Don't worry about it. Getting the push now wouldn't bother me.'

She certainly didn't look worried as she stood there smiling down at Amy. A moment later and she was gone, off to her despised job near Bodmin that she would be glad to leave.

15

Callum had left by the time Amy had driven herself and Rufus back to Penmarrow.

'Callum had things to do,' Jim said as she joined him in Reception, holding Rufus on his lead. Everything looked just the same, apart from the door being wedged open. A glance round assured her that the paintings were still in position. She wondered that Jim didn't mention them.

Jim bent to pat Rufus, who wriggled his pleasure. 'Would you like to take him round to the house? Maria would like to see you.'

'Of course. But you know that we're expecting a client to turn up this morning, a Mr Robert Jones? He's a lover of storms and gales.'

'Then he'll like it here. He phoned just minutes ago to say he'll be late. A fallen tree across the road, apparently.'

Amy smiled, though it wasn't funny.

'Just so,' said Jim, his eyes twinkling. 'I'll shut up here for the next hour. But first I have something to do.' He gestured towards the canvases. 'This lot have got to go.'

'Gabriel Ward's work,' she said. 'He'll be back for them.'

'And the sooner the better. Meanwhile, they can be stacked over there. A worse mass of wasted paint I've yet to see.'

'I'm sorry.'

'No harm done, my dear, as long as I don't have to look at them.'

'I'll help you.'

'That's better,' Jim said when the job was done. 'Let's go. I don't like the sound of that wind.'

Maria was there at the door to welcome them, the shoulder of her uninjured arm holding it open. Rufus licked her good hand, obviously pleased to see her.

'And how's Jim's sister now?' Amy said.

Maria ran her hand through her wispy grey hair. 'Brenda? Feeling the strain of the journey a bit, poor Brenda. She managed to get upstairs, but I'm wondering now whether or not we shouldn't have tried to fix up a bed for her down here.' She looked round, pursing her lips.

Amy could see why. The kitchen was narrow, and it would hardly have done as a bedroom anyway.

'Now, Amy, you'd like some coffee?' Maria said, full of concern.

'Only if you let me make it.'

'A determined young lady, aren't you?'

'A practical one,' Jim said, shrugging himself out of his jacket.

Maria smiled. 'And so like Selina.'

Amy was surprised. Growing up, she and her sister had never looked alike, but now she supposed there must be some family resemblance.

'Would you mind . . . I mean, I'm really anxious. May I use your phone first?'

They didn't mind, of course, and Jim showed her where it was in the hall.

Mark's mobile was answered at once by a woman's low voice. 'Can I help you?'

'I . . . I . . . I'm trying to contact Mark. Mark Downley. It's his phone. I'm Amy. Where is he? I'd like to speak to him. Are you Lara?'

'Lara Webster? Not me.' She laughed at the idea. 'I picked up this mobile, and had no idea whose it was. Lara lives down the road. She'll be able to get it back to him if they're both still here.'

'Not there? But where . . . ?'

'Who knows? I think they went off somewhere the day before yesterday, but I'm not sure.'

Amy mumbled something incoherent and clicked off. Over on the islands, Mark's mobile was his lifeline. His carelessness was astounding. Bemused, she returned to the kitchen. She had spoken to someone on the islands who wasn't Mark. And, come to think of it, she didn't know who this person was.

And where was she exactly? She had said that Lara lived down the road. Brouma had no roads, or anything much else for that matter.

'Any good?' asked Jim.

'Someone's found his mobile and . . .'

She broke off at the sound of chattering outside, and then a tap on the door. Jim ushered Grace and Belinda Allardyce inside, and shut the door firmly behind them at a sudden gust of wind.

'We've come to ask after the patient,' Grace said, smiling. 'So you didn't leave us after all, Amy dear?'

'You're just in time for coffee,' Jim said.

There was a tremendous crash. A huge blast of wind shook the place, followed by a loud roar and a cracking sound, as if the world had gone mad.

Amy clutched the back of a chair. From upstairs came a panicky shout.

'I'm coming, Brenda,' Jim shouted.

They others looked at each other in alarm. For a moment, no one moved. The noise had stopped so suddenly that the ensuing silence was uncanny. And then Jim was back.

'We might have been out in that,' Grace whispered.

'We need that coffee,' Jim said.

* * *

The damage outside was considerable. Amy could hardly believe the devastation when at last she and Jim ventured out. They had left the three women in Brenda's room, peering out of the window at the swathes of depleted trees. Beyond, Amy could see shattered caravans, one overturned. Tiles from the roof of the Reception building littered the ground.

'It's horrible,' she murmured, weak at the knees. 'Unbelievable.'

Jim stared in silence.

Amy could see now that not all the caravans were wrecked. Some had sustained only a little damage, and others were still in position, looking gaunt and lonely.

'Thank goodness no one was in any

of the caravans,' she said.

She glanced down at the Allardyces' and saw that it was still there, but not the one she had prepared for Mr Robert Jones who loved storms.

'It looks as if a huge squall swept up through here and we caught it full on,' said Jim. 'We'd better check the phone in Reception to see if the lines are down.'

Almost immediately, Stella was there, looking askance at the dereliction.

'You've a job on your hands here,' she said.

'And we're expecting a client at any moment,' Amy said.

But it seemed their new guest had already arrived. He was coming jauntily up the steps, a rucksack on his shoulder. He dropped it to the floor with a thud.

'Robert!'

'Stella, by all that's wonderful. Good to see you. I thought you might not be around anymore.'

'In the churchyard, you mean?'

His laugh was deep and throaty. 'Good old Stella, as large as life. Well done.'

'So what are you doing here?'

'Storm watching, what else? I'll be painting storm scenes from now on. My oils and brushes are in the car.' He slipped his arms out of his rucksack. 'I'm ready to help as and when. But I won't be a nuisance. I'll go off and book in somewhere or other for tonight.'

Amy caught the expression on Stella's face and wondered.

* * *

An hour later, Amy was alone in Reception, checking through the bookings ledger, when the clatter and roar of the van alerted her to the arrival of the two people she was dreading. Where was Jim when he was needed? But this was her concern, and she would deal with it on her own.

The doors of the van burst open. Amy stood up and waited. Gabriel entered, his long hair dishevelled. Phoebe, behind him, hesitated in the open doorway; and then, seeing that the place was a dog-free zone today, came purposely inside.

'We want his paintings,' she said. 'If any have been damaged in the storm, we'll sue.'

Amy smiled. 'You've chosen a reasonable hour to come for them this time.'

'We were leaving. We needed them.'

'That's no excuse. As I told you, I had no key to let you in. I was given no warning of your departure time.'

'Or us of yours, either.'

'Your break-in could be a criminal charge if the owner decides to report it,' Amy said with spirit.

'What?' Gabriel's face reddened so that his scar showed up, an angry white line.

Amy gripped the edge of the desk. 'You heard me.'

'Criminal charge?' Phoebe spat out. 'That dog attacked me! I could have you for that, having a dangerous dog about the place.'

'Take the paintings and go.'

Tight-lipped, Phoebe glared at her brother.

'Are you letting her get away with this?'

'I want my work,' he said.

'Take them,' said Amy. 'Except that one.' She pointed to the painting on the bookstand. 'That one stays right here until the bill for the damage to the broken lock has been settled in full. The bill will come to you in due course.'

Gabriel nodded. He looked thoroughly chastened, and Amy couldn't help but feel sorry for him as he got his pile of paintings outside.

Phoebe, though, was another matter. She seemed fixed to the spot, standing there in her flowing clothes, gripping her canvas bag close to her as if she expected Amy to snatch it out of her hands. As Gabriel picked up the last of the pile, she turned on her heel and followed him.

'You'll hear more of this,' she snarled back.

'I hope so,' Amy called after her. 'The

bill paid in full.'

Suddenly, she noticed Jim standing near the bottom of the steps, unnoticed by the pair getting into their battered van and slamming the doors. The gears crashed and they were off.

'Well done, my dear,' Jim said, joining Amy.

She gave a shaky laugh. 'You heard?'

'Every word. An unpleasant couple.'

'It's the sister who's the trouble.'

'You have a soft heart, my dear. They can count themselves lucky they got away with it so lightly. But I think we'll have the better of the bargain if he doesn't pay up. That painting on the stand is the best of the lot.'

'You liked them?' She was astonished.

'Not at all.' He pointed his stick at it. 'But I've a feeling it could be worth a lot.'

'Yes.'

'Ah well, that's as may be. Our new guest is going to be an improvement on those two. Thank you, my dear, for making him welcome.'

'I think it was Stella who did that.'

'Now, how about you take Rufus for a short walk? No point in staying here with the phone line down, so we'll close up now. We've pizza from the freezer for the six of us. You'll join us?'

She smiled. 'That sounds good. Thanks.'

The encounter with the Wards, and the effort to remain calm and in control, had left her feeling drained. She made sure her jacket was zipped as high as it would go, and then set off with Rufus, down past the damaged caravans towards the gap in the wall that gave access to the cliff path.

At the gap, she hesitated, but Rufus was eager to go through.

'Sorry, Rufus,' she said.

But she was tempted. Down there on that beautiful little beach it would surely be sheltered. *In her dreams!* She had only to look at the sea rushing into the cliff to know how foolish that was.

* * *

There wouldn't be much beach showing at the moment. She stayed there for
some time, watching the heaving sea.
The salty breeze was restorative, and
she took deep breaths of it. Then,
reluctantly, she turned back.

16

'Where's Amy?'

Callum, at the door of the house, spun round as he heard her approach. He looked businesslike in his waterproof jacket, but his voice was uncertain.

They looked at each other in silence.

'Just in time for lunch with us, Callum,' came Maria's gentle voice. 'You're very welcome. There's plenty here for all.'

'I didn't know where you were,' Callum murmured as he followed Amy into the kitchen, warm with the smells of cooking pizza. 'I saw your car covered with fallen branches. I couldn't see you anywhere.'

'I was here in the house,' she said. 'Grace and Belinda were here too. We were all safe.'

'I couldn't get through on the phone. I had to come as soon as I could.'

'And then Rufus needed a walk.'

The dog pricked his ears up at the sound of his name, but Callum gazed down at him unseeingly.

'Are you all right, Amy?'

'Not good,' she admitted.

He looked grave as they removed their outer garments. 'I thought not.'

Jim's stick clattered to the floor unheeded.

'Glad to see you, Callum,' he said heartily. 'Maria's laid an extra space. Have you a moment before we eat?'

Callum, looking at Amy, hesitated for a moment, and then he followed Jim from the room.

'It's just a bit of business that needs sorting out, Amy,' Maria said. 'They won't be long.'

The men were back almost immediately, and during the meal, Amy was content to let the others do the talking while she listened to the silence outside. Sleeping soundly on his beanbag now, Rufus was oblivious to what was going on around him. There was something soothing in his quiet breathing. It felt good, too, to have Callum here with them.

She thought of Mark, whose mobile had been found by someone who knew Lara. No hope now that he could contact her. She put her knife and fork down.

'Not hungry, dear?' said Grace in concern.

Amy shook her head.

'It's the shock,' Belinda said. She took another mouthful and ate it appreciatively.

'And of course you're in shock, too, Maria dear,' said Grace. 'We'll get back to our caravan now we know it's still there, and leave you in peace.'

'I'll come with you,' said Jim, getting up and reaching for his stick. 'I need to check on the safety factor and see that all's well. We don't want it collapsing about your heads.'

Amy was surprised that Callum didn't offer to go too.

'We'll see to the washing up,' he said when Jim and the two ladies had retrieved their coats and were ready to set off. Maria, smiling her thanks, retreated upstairs.

When it was done, Callum placed the last of the dinner plates in the rack and turned to face Amy, to broach the subject that was uppermost in his mind.

'I've made enquiries over there on the islands. That's what I came to tell you, Amy. There's been good business in renting small boats this last week or two, and they've all been returned.'

'I see.' She picked up the plate and began to dry it.

'There is no one on Brouma now.'

'You're sure of that?'

'My contact over there checked for me. No reports of accidents, either, but who knows? You haven't heard anything more?'

'Mark's mobile's been found,' she said. 'Picked up somewhere. I phoned, and this person told me. She's a friend of someone who knows Mark, but she can't give it back. She doesn't know where they are.'

'Does she think he's left the islands?'

'She's not sure.'

'Unfinished business,' Callum said. 'Something has to be done about it.'

She had thought that herself, but then pushed the thought to the back of her mind. She looked at him in silence.

'I've made an online booking for the next sailing of the *Scillonian*, since I have business over there that I can bring forward. That should be Monday, the day after tomorrow. The booking is for two.'

Amy had no need to ask him who the two bookings were for. His expression left no doubt that he had her in mind. She bit her lip, aware she seemed ungrateful in her strange reluctance to accept.

'I . . . I'm not too sure that it's the best thing for me to do,' she said.

'Think about it,' he said.

She nodded. Yes, she would think about it. The booking wasn't until Monday. There was the rest of today and all of Sunday to get through first.

Unfinished business, she thought later, when Callum had left. He was right, of course. She had to know that Mark was safe, but she understood now with certainty that concern for his welfare no longer meant that she cared for him in the same way that she had for these last few months. She needed to know that no harm had come to him before she could get on with her life. She would help out here for as long as Jim and Maria needed her, and then she would be free to leave Penmarrow as soon as transport could be arranged.

* * *

The firm that Jim contacted for the removal of the damaged caravans confirmed they would be on the spot as soon as they were given the go-ahead. Even though it was Sunday, next day the locksmith arrived soon after break-fast, and so did Robert Jones, eager to get cracking on removing the fallen branches.

Amy had already prepared a caravan for his occupancy, urged on by Jim, who was anxious to fulfil his contract with Robert and not let him down.

'I've never had a holiday on a bombsite before,' he said cheerfully. 'A new experience, and I'm all for that.'

He threw himself with vigour into clearing fallen branches and other debris caused by the storm. Amy's car was a write-off, but the Allardyces' vehicle had escaped damage, and that was good.

Now that the wind had dropped, Amy even considered taking Rufus down to the small beach down below; but, out with him on the cliff path again, she could see that white crests were still decorating the sea further out, and the breakers rushing in were alarmingly high. She wondered if the masses of seaweed she had seen there the other day had been washed away by now.

They ambled on for the longest walk Rufus had managed since his operation.

* * *

'A visitor for you, Amy,' Jim greeted her when she walked up the slope towards Reception.

'A visitor?' she said in surprise. Jim wouldn't have announced Callum's arrival in this way, or Stella's.

'I think it's your young man.'

'Mark?'

'I'll be busy at the house for the next half-hour or so, my dear.'

Mark, here in Penmarrow? How could this be?

The same Mark, exuding self-confidence, standing there with his legs slightly apart and smiling as if he expected an exuberant welcome!

'You're safe?' She struggled to disguise the tremor in her voice, but couldn't quite manage it. 'Are you all right?' Of course he was all right. Never better, by the look of him, glowing with satisfaction.

'Why shouldn't I be? I've done some excellent work over there, Amy. Really good. But the plans have changed.'

He looked down at Rufus, who was sniffing his legs, and pushed him away with one foot.

'And this is the dog, I suppose, that caused all the trouble?'

Amy's knees felt weak and she moved to the steps to lean on the handrail.

'I kept trying to contact you, Mark. I was worried sick.'

'Lara was brilliant, coming up with all sorts of ideas for shots that really worked.'

'Then someone found your phone.'

'I lost it on St Mary's. That's why I couldn't phone you.'

She let that go, but it must have sounded a weak excuse even to his ears.

'You went back to Brouma?'

'No, no.' He sounded impatient. 'Isn't there somewhere we can go to talk in this god-forsaken place?'

The locksmith had done his job, but the door to Reception was unlocked. He followed her in and looked round.

'Bit of a mess everywhere, isn't there?'

She almost offered him coffee, but thought better of it. What had to be said was better to be done quickly.

'We got the last plane out.'

'Before the gales? But that was . . . '

'I know. We were lucky.'

'We?' She knew the answer, but she had to hear it from him, although it didn't sound as if he wanted to tell her.

'When we knew the forecast for the south-west was bad, we got going as fast as we could. Broke a few speed records getting to London, though. I've got another commission, Amy. Isn't that great?'

His smug tone was almost more than she could bear. She took a deep, painful breath.

'I thought you'd be in some sort of trouble, Mark. I didn't know what to do.'

'You must have known we couldn't go on as we were, Amy. I didn't mean it to end like this.' He sounded regretful now. 'I'm sorry, Amy, really I am. I don't know what to say, but . . . '

'And that girl, Lara. Is she with you?'

'Not yet. She's back there in Bodmin. I'm getting back there straight away, and then we'll head home.' Again, the smug tone of voice. 'I want us to stay friends, Amy. We'll stay friends, won't we?'

Friends, she thought. Your *friends* didn't disregard your feelings as Mark had done. And he was going to be with Lara, who didn't sound the sort of friend she wanted, either. Friendship was a deeply satisfying relationship, and there wouldn't be any of that from either of them.

'Friends, Mark? I don't think so.' She was proud of her smile, but it was an effort.

He looked surprised, then relieved.

There seemed nothing more to be said after that.

For the rest of the morning, she went about her self-imposed duties in a daze. On one level, she could think only of the paintings that Gabriel had taken away, paintings that caught the eye and made you look at them because of the vibrancy in the way he had used the oils.

She hadn't yet seen any of Robert Jones' work, but suspected he had talent. Storms and gales, she thought, imagining great swathes of torrential rain and trees bending with the force of the wind, and wondering how he could portray all that in a way that would appeal to others. Maybe she would soon find out. Stella would know. She had known him years ago, and it seemed that he remembered her with fondness.

Would she ever get to the stage when she remembered Mark with fondness? They had had some good times together. She thought of an outing to Polesden Lacey, for him to take some photographs he hoped would be taken by a local magazine. On the strength of that, Mark had taken her for a meal down at an expensive place near the river, and they had walked beneath the willow trees, hand in hand. But even then, now she came to think of it, he had been preoccupied with the next subject he would choose to photograph, and could talk of little else.

On another, deeper level, she felt a dark and confused sadness that their loving friendship had ended on what seemed to her to be a sour note. She needed something else to bring closure in a more satisfactory way. Ending a relationship was never easy.

★   ★   ★

Stella tried to force herself to stay away from Penmarrow, in case her jubilation was too obvious whilst the place was a shambles. But this wasn't fair to Amy, who had enough to contend with without wondering why someone she clearly thought of as a friend had deserted her.

She was a true home bird and, if these latest plans came to fruition, she would never be away from the area again. And neither would Jason, she suspected. He was more like her than he was prepared to admit. These family genes came out in such unexpected ways. He had come home a couple of weeks ago with the scheme that had seemed, then, to be completely harebrained, but it had set her thinking. It had set Jason thinking, too, about what he wanted from life. Dog breeding. Who would have thought it?

But she mustn't allow Amy to have the slightest inkling. This was on Callum's orders. There were other, more important, issues for Amy to work out that must take precedence over a venue for a new art gallery to be run by her.

Sunday morning was, in any case, as good a time as any to start sorting out some of the stuff that had accumulated in her small cottage since the time she had been here, and which she didn't want cluttering up her new home. By afternoon she had a couple of bin liners outside the back door, stuffed full of old magazines and brochures for dog maintenance items she was astonished she had kept.

She had just taken another, smaller

bag of rubbish outside when she saw Amy coming along the cliff path.

'No Rufus?' she called.

'Resting after his walk,' Amy said. 'I need to see Callum urgently.'

'He's not here. He's down at the sailing club overseeing the clear-up. One or two of the undamaged boats are out on the water.'

Amy turned to look. Yes, there they were, white sails moving fast on the ruffled sea.

'A bit hairy out there,' Stella said. 'Sorts the men from the boys. Come in anyway. Coffee?'

'You're busy.'

'Just a bit of a clear-out.'

'You look as if you're moving house.'

'Could be. Not for a while, though. Callum has plans to make the three cottages into one.'

'And he'd throw you out?' Amy said, surprised.

'Not really. There have been talks. I can't say more. I promised.'

'You said you were no good at

keeping secrets.'

'I said that?' Stella said. *Button your lips, you silly woman.*

Amy smiled. 'Then I won't keep you. Any news of Gabriel and Phoebe?'

'Ha!' said Stella, relieved at this distraction. 'He still wants an exhibition space in the area. He was keen to get hold of the cottage next door because of those outbuildings out at the back.'

'A perfect location,' said Amy.

'But not for Gabriel,' Stella said firmly. 'For someone else nearer home. Jason's idea, of course.'

Then, horrified, she clamped her hand to her mouth.

'I've done it now, haven't I?'

17

Amy was still pondering Stella's strange words as she went down the path to the village. The beach beckoned: a last chance, perhaps, to wander across it and enjoy the feeling of space and freedom she had felt the first time she had come here with Stella.

The boats were coming back in now, and she stood and watched their owners retrieve their launching trolleys and heave their boats up the beach. One or two stopped to adjust something or other, calling out remarks to others as they passed. A cheerful, bustling scene of sudden activity. She saw Callum among them, and at that moment he saw her too.

He waved. 'Give me a few minutes and I'll be with you,' he called. Good health radiated from him as he stood there in his shorts and navy sweater, and Amy felt a pang of longing she struggled to suppress.

A wooden bench nearby made the perfect resting place, and she was glad to wait here in the sunshine for a short while.

'So, you're enjoying a bit of free time?' Callum greeted her.

'There's something I have to tell you, Callum.'

He said nothing as he sat down on the seat beside her. Had he guessed, she wondered, and would he now cancel the *Scillonian* booking because it would be more convenient for him to stick to his original work programme?

She cleared her throat.

'Mark came to see me at Penmarrow.'

Callum swung round to face her. 'He did? So he's no longer languishing on some island, expecting you to turn up?'

'He's safe. That's all that matters.'

'All?'

She flushed. 'Perhaps not all.'

'It wouldn't be if I got my hands on him.'

She gave a shaky laugh. 'It won't come to that.'

'Well, I'm pleased and relieved for you, Amy. So all your worrying was in vain?'

Amy nodded, unable to speak for a moment.

'And? Did he say why he hadn't contacted you before the telephone line went down?'

'There was no need. I knew. Deep down, I knew. And I realised, quite suddenly, that I was glad. He's gone out of my life now, for good.'

He said nothing, but a small tic moved at the side of his mouth.

'I must get back,' she said, standing up. 'There's a lot to do. Jim looks so tired and worried.'

Callum got up too, and they began to walk back across the beach.

'His son will be home soon,' he said. 'And, of course, your sister. There will be a lot to discuss. Jim and Maria know they can't carry on here much longer, even if there wasn't his sister to consider.'

'They'd give up Penmarrow?'

'They think it will come to that.'

'But where will they go?'

'They think a bungalow would be sensible, somewhere on level ground. There's one likely to come up in the area in the next month or two.'

Amy thought of the caravans left standing that were old and needing replacing, and of the lack of amenities on the site. Huge capital would be needed to make it a going concern, and a prospective purchaser might be difficult to find.

'I'm not sure it's a good time to put a place like Penmarrow on the market,' she said.

'There's someone interested near at hand.'

She looked at him in surprise, names ringing through her head. Gabriel, Phoebe, the Allardyce sisters? Robert Jones, perhaps, newly retired. But running a caravan site would hardly leave much time to paint, and that seemed to be his aim in life. Or Jason, who wanted to live in a place with a view?

'I can see I've amused you,' Callum said.

'It seems too good to be true if they want to sell.'

'That's what Stella thinks.'

She stopped in surprise. 'Surely not Stella?'

Impossible to think of Stella spending hours in Reception; sorting out problems; arranging for the cleaning of caravans; being there to welcome clients.

He smiled. 'If planning permission is granted, I'm prepared to lend her the money for the purchase.'

'But . . . '

'You look dismayed.'

'Stella running Penmarrow?'

'Not a bit of it. The set-up could be ideal for what she wants to do. I've reason to believe it will go through because livestock was once kept here. Dog kennels wouldn't be so much different. A change of use for the place to revert to how it was years ago.'

'So it's not the Allardyce sisters who are purchasing the place? I was beginning to wonder. Or Jason?'

'It was Jason's idea. He's hoping Stella will take him on as kennel-lad. But it's all in the future. Something to work towards, to plan for and to dream about.'

Something to dream about — yes, that was it, she thought. That was what everyone needed. She thought of the vast basement beneath the house that would be useful for something or other too. An artist's studio? Who knew?

'So, our day out on the islands is no longer an option,' Callum said.

'No.'

'It's the last place you will want to be, bringing back unhappiness and regret and goodness knows what.'

They started to walk again. Out on the horizon clouds were forming. *The changeable Cornish weather,* Amy thought. Soon, the sunshine would have gone, the cliffs dimmed in the gloomy light. But then she saw a glimmer of bright-ness beneath the clouds; and, as she watched, it spread until all sign of the gloom had gone. How could this be in such a short time?

'All I needed to know was that Mark was safe,' she said.

'All?'

'I wouldn't lie to you, Callum.'

Mark was in the past, gone from her life; and she felt an uplifting of spirits, as if the clouds had gone from her life, too.

'I don't want to waste those two tickets.' Callum sounded less confident now, vulnerable even. Then he brightened. 'Eddie Knowlton will be on board — the naturalist — doing wildlife-spotting.'

'On board the *Scillonian*?'

'He goes across on a regular basis for research purposes. I happen to know he'll be there on Monday, even though spotting anything is doubtful because of the recent storm.'

For a moment, Amy thought of someone checking the distant Brouma. But that had nothing to do with this.

'What does he expect to see?'

'Hopes, not expects. Who knows . . . dolphins, porpoises? He even spotted a Minke whale once. In much calmer conditions, of course.'

'Sounds good.'

'If you like that sort of thing. Ah well, with luck, I can find someone else to go with me. Let me see . . . Stella, perhaps.'

'Hardly. She's too far busy throwing things out.'

'Jason, then.'

'Won't he be at work?'

'So, who shall I take instead?'

She looked at him standing there, his bright hair ruffled by the breeze that was beginning to die down now. It seemed important to her that she should answer before it completely subsided.

'Can I come with you?' she said.

'Even when there's no Mark to meet?'

'Especially because of that.'

'So it must be the thought of seeing dolphins, then?'

She smiled.

'If you say so. And seeing for myself those silver beaches and turquoise sea I've heard so much about.'

He laughed, and she laughed too. A feeling of coming home swept over her, safety and belonging and the urge to stay in this loving moment forever.

For a moment, he didn't move; then he took her in his arms and she melted against him, raising her face. The love she saw in his eyes was beautiful as he bent and kissed her.

* * *

Early next morning, as the dawn chorus filled the air with music, the Allardyce sisters tapped gently on Amy's caravan door. Both looked expectant as she opened it. Grace was carrying a small parcel wrapped in tissue paper, and Belinda held out a large brown envelope.

'For you, dear,' Grace said as they gave them to her.

Almost overcome, Amy took the gifts and looked down at them wonderingly.

'You're good friends,' she murmured.

'We'll help look after Rufus while you're away,' Belinda said gruffly.

'But now we won't delay you,' said Grace. 'A good voyage, my dear, and may we wish you every happiness.'

With her heart full she watched them depart. Then she closed the door and unwrapped the gifts they had brought her. Belinda's was a portrait of a dog easily recognisable as Rufus. She had caught the soulful expression in his brown eyes to perfection. The silver photograph frame that was Grace's present was exactly right to show the painting off to its best advantage. *Such thoughtful gifts from thoughtful people*, she mused as she disposed of the wrappings and placed the framed painting on the worktop to greet her on her return.

Instead of simply a day out with Callum, it felt as if she were going on a long, important journey — and perhaps she was, metaphorically speaking. A journey from which she would return changed forever. The fanciful thought seemed to have transferred itself from Grace and Belinda to herself — but who knew? They understood that it was a significant time for her, and because of that she was prepared to believe it.

She climbed into Callum's Land Rover and they set off.

'You're silent, my love,' said Callum as they joined the main road. 'You're not regretting anything?'

'How could I?'

'Only if that chap was still getting under your skin.'

'I think someone else is doing that now.'

'Wonderful. As long as that person is me.'

'It always will be.'

'For me too,' he said. 'I see marriage, children, a happy and fulfilled life together.'

Simple words said with conviction from a man she loved and trusted.

* * *

And there was the *Scillonian*, waiting at her berth with sunshine illuminating her white paint. For a moment Amy stared at the proud vessel waiting for them. A symbol of optimism, she thought, a setting out on the sea for those islands, and then the return to Pentowle with the one who meant the whole world to her. An adventure, yes, and she couldn't ask for anything more.

Callum seemed to feel it too. He turned to her, his eyes shining. 'All set, then?'

'Very much so.'

'That's my girl.' He took her arm and squeezed it.

Then, together, they walked up the gangway.

We do hope that you have enjoyed reading this large print book.

Did you know that all of our titles are available for purchase?

We publish a wide range of high quality large print books including:
Romances, Mysteries, Classics
General Fiction
Non Fiction and Westerns

Special interest titles available in large print are:
The Little Oxford Dictionary
Music Book, Song Book
Hymn Book, Service Book

Also available from us courtesy of Oxford University Press:
Young Readers' Dictionary
(large print edition)
Young Readers' Thesaurus
(large print edition)

For further information or a free brochure, please contact us at:
Ulverscroft Large Print Books Ltd.,
The Green, Bradgate Road, Anstey,
Leicester, LE7 7FU, England.
Tel: (00 44) 0116 236 4325
Fax: (00 44) 0116 234 0205

RETURN TO RIVER SPRINGS

Charlotte McFall

Nine years ago Georgia left River Springs, vowing never to return. But now she's back to start a new job — only to discover that the secrets of her past will not stay buried. Before she has a chance to reconcile with her old flame, Detective Justin Rose, an accident lands her daughter in hospital; and when morning comes, the little girl is nowhere to be found. With her life falling apart around her, and Justin demanding answers she doesn't want to give, Georgia begins the desperate search for her daughter . . .